Sir Arthur Conan Doyle's
The **Adventure** of
the **Solitary Cyclist**

Adapted by: Vincent Goodwin

Illustrated by: Ben Dunn

magic
wagon

visit us at
www.abdopublishing.com

Graphic Planet™ is a trademark and logo of Magic Wagon.

Printed in the United States of America, North Mankato, Minnesota.
022012
092012
 This book contains at least 10% recycled materials.

Written by Sir Arthur Conan Doyle
Adapted by Vincent Goodwin
Illustrated by Ben Dunn
Colored by Robby Bevard
Lettered by Doug Dlin
Edited by Stephanie Hedlund and Rochelle Baltzer
Interior layout by Antarctic Press
Cover art by Ben Dunn
Cover design by Abbey Fitzgerald

Library of Congress Cataloging-in-Publication Data

Goodwin, Vincent.
  Sir Arthur Conan Doyle's The adventure of the solitary cyclist / adapted by Vincent Goodwin ; illustrated by Ben Dunn.
     p. cm. -- (The graphic novel adventures of Sherlock Holmes)
  Summary: Retold in graphic novel form, Sherlock Holmes investigates the mysterious bearded man who is following Miss Violet Smith on a bicycle.
  ISBN 978-1-61641-894-6
  1. Doyle, Arthur Conan, Sir, 1859-1930. Adventure of the solitary cyclist--Adaptations. 2. Holmes, Sherlock (Fictitious character)--Comic books, strips, etc. 3. Holmes, Sherlock (Fictitious character)--Juvenile fiction. 4. Graphic novels. [1. Graphic novels. 2. Doyle, Arthur Conan, Sir, 1859-1930. Adventure of the solitary cyclist--Adaptations. 3. Mystery and detective stories.] I. Dunn, Ben, ill. II. Doyle, Arthur Conan, Sir, 1859-1930. Adventure of the solitary cyclist. III. Title. IV. Title: Adventure of the solitary cyclist. V. Series: Goodwin, Vincent. Graphic novel adventures of Sherlock Holmes.
  PZ7.7.G66Sirm 2012
  741.5'973--dc23
                                                                 2011052262

Table of Contents

Cast

Sherlock Holmes

Dr. John Watson

Miss Violet Smith

Mrs. Smith

Mr. Robert Carruthers

Mr. Jack Woodley

Mr. Williamson

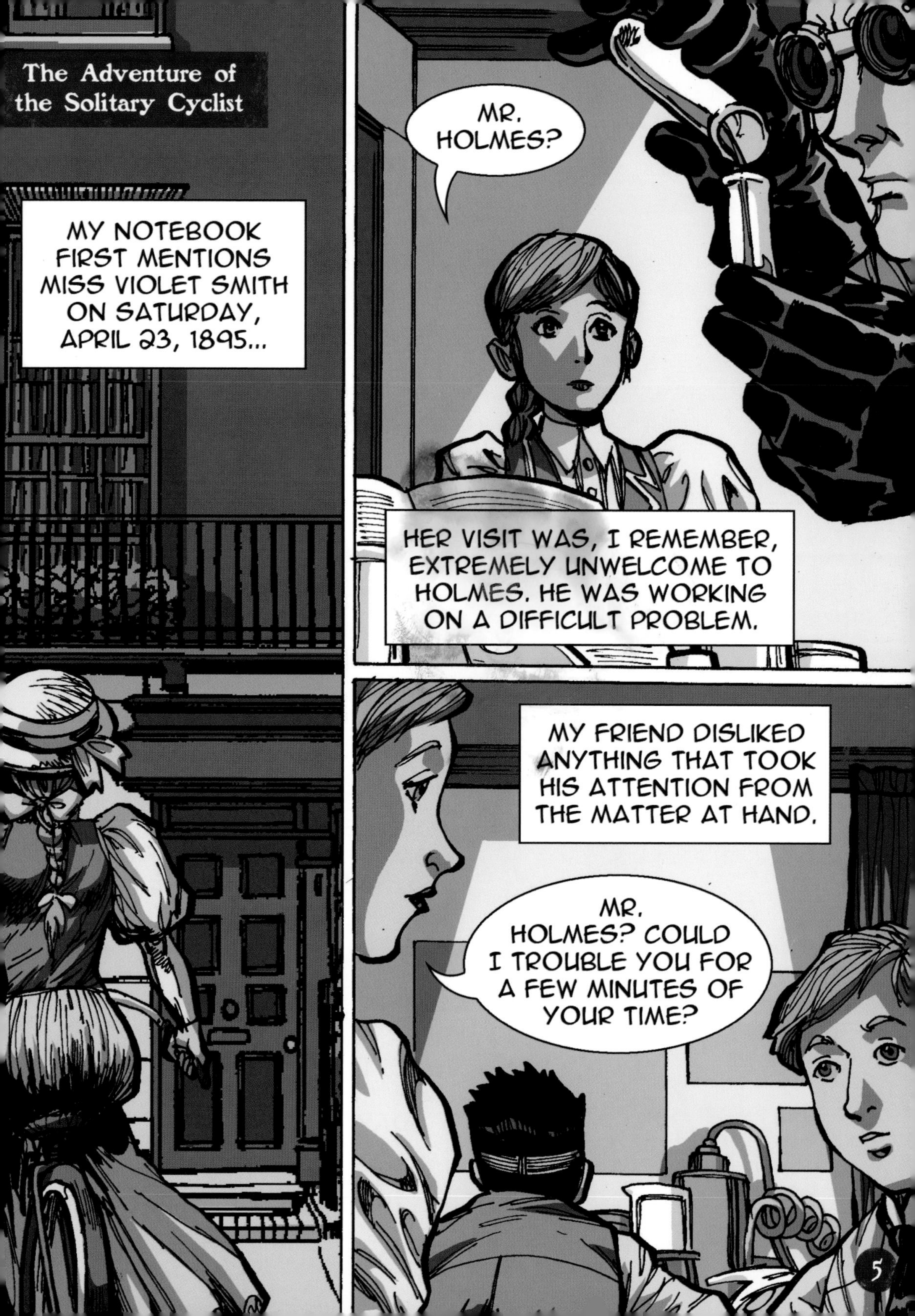
The Adventure of the Solitary Cyclist
MY NOTEBOOK FIRST MENTIONS MISS VIOLET SMITH ON SATURDAY, APRIL 23, 1895...
MR. HOLMES?
HER VISIT WAS, I REMEMBER, EXTREMELY UNWELCOME TO HOLMES. HE WAS WORKING ON A DIFFICULT PROBLEM.
MY FRIEND DISLIKED ANYTHING THAT TOOK HIS ATTENTION FROM THE MATTER AT HAND.
MR. HOLMES? COULD I TROUBLE YOU FOR A FEW MINUTES OF YOUR TIME?

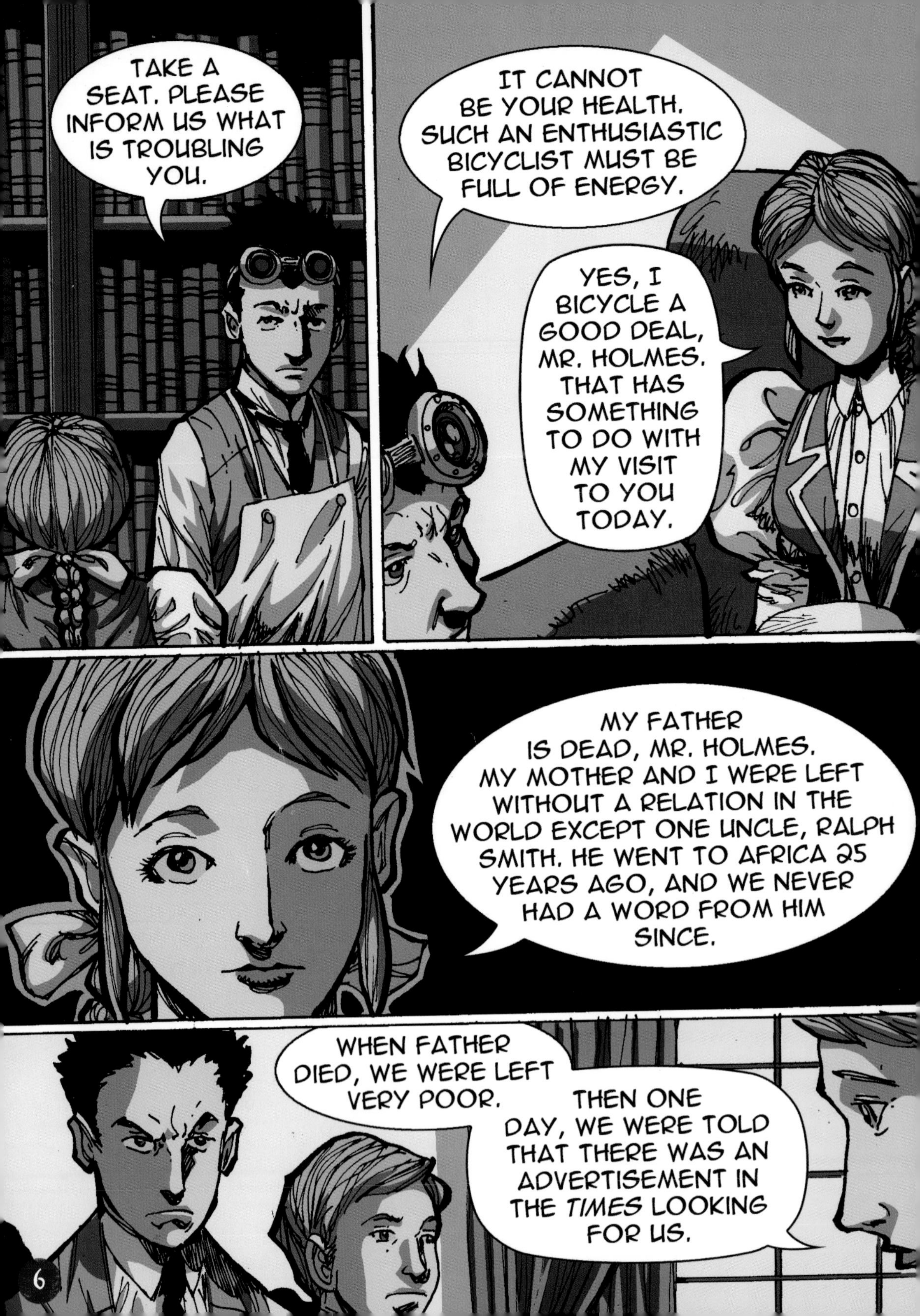
TAKE A SEAT. PLEASE INFORM US WHAT IS TROUBLING YOU.
IT CANNOT BE YOUR HEALTH. SUCH AN ENTHUSIASTIC BICYCLIST MUST BE FULL OF ENERGY.
YES, I BICYCLE A GOOD DEAL, MR. HOLMES. THAT HAS SOMETHING TO DO WITH MY VISIT TO YOU TODAY.
MY FATHER IS DEAD, MR. HOLMES. MY MOTHER AND I WERE LEFT WITHOUT A RELATION IN THE WORLD EXCEPT ONE UNCLE, RALPH SMITH. HE WENT TO AFRICA 25 YEARS AGO, AND WE NEVER HAD A WORD FROM HIM SINCE.
WHEN FATHER DIED, WE WERE LEFT VERY POOR.
THEN ONE DAY, WE WERE TOLD THAT THERE WAS AN ADVERTISEMENT IN THE *TIMES* LOOKING FOR US.

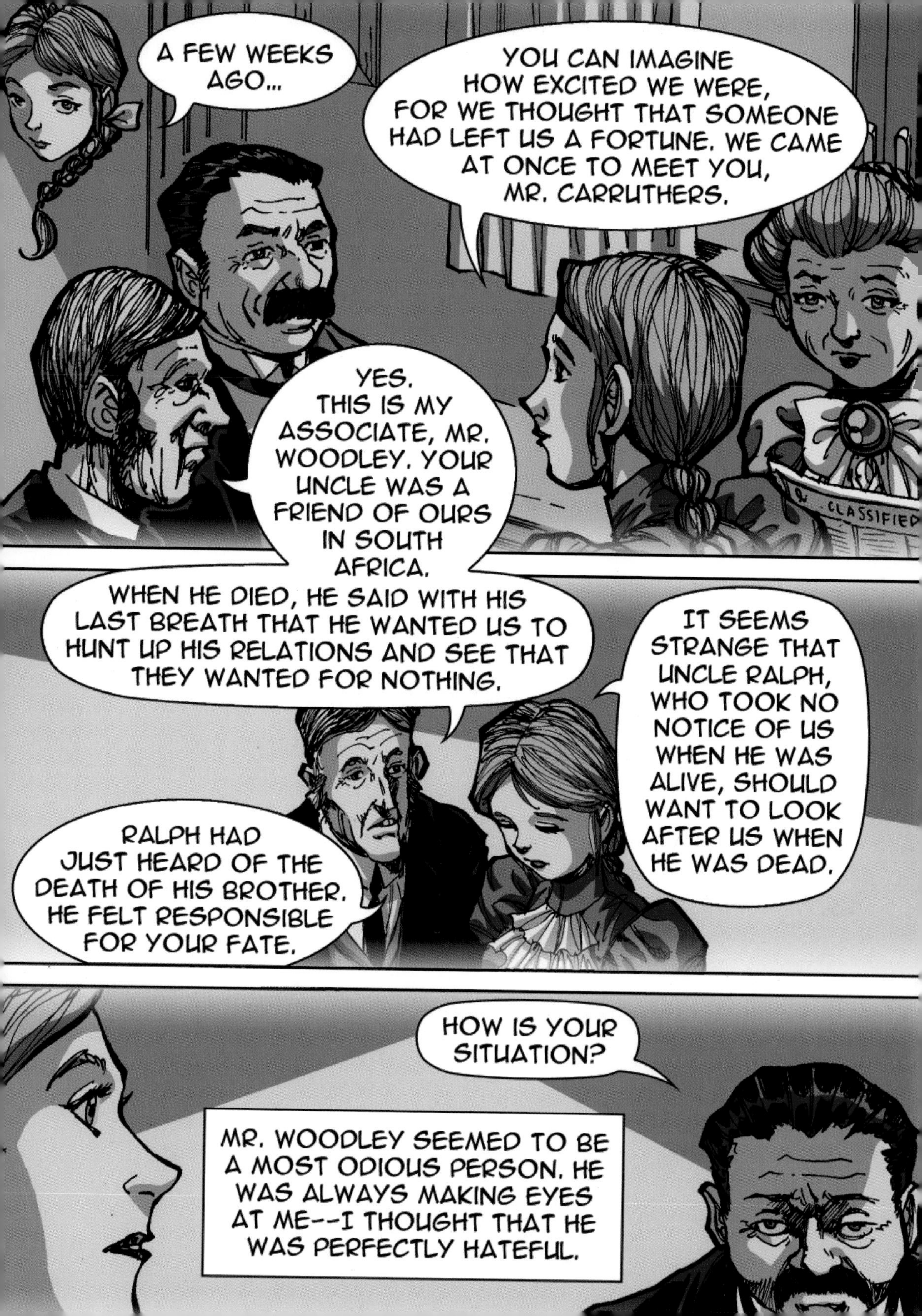
A FEW WEEKS AGO...
YOU CAN IMAGINE HOW EXCITED WE WERE, FOR WE THOUGHT THAT SOMEONE HAD LEFT US A FORTUNE. WE CAME AT ONCE TO MEET YOU, MR. CARRUTHERS.
YES. THIS IS MY ASSOCIATE, MR. WOODLEY. YOUR UNCLE WAS A FRIEND OF OURS IN SOUTH AFRICA.
CLASSIFIED
WHEN HE DIED, HE SAID WITH HIS LAST BREATH THAT HE WANTED US TO HUNT UP HIS RELATIONS AND SEE THAT THEY WANTED FOR NOTHING.
IT SEEMS STRANGE THAT UNCLE RALPH, WHO TOOK NO NOTICE OF US WHEN HE WAS ALIVE, SHOULD WANT TO LOOK AFTER US WHEN HE WAS DEAD.
RALPH HAD JUST HEARD OF THE DEATH OF HIS BROTHER. HE FELT RESPONSIBLE FOR YOUR FATE.
HOW IS YOUR SITUATION?
MR. WOODLEY SEEMED TO BE A MOST ODIOUS PERSON. HE WAS ALWAYS MAKING EYES AT ME--I THOUGHT THAT HE WAS PERFECTLY HATEFUL.

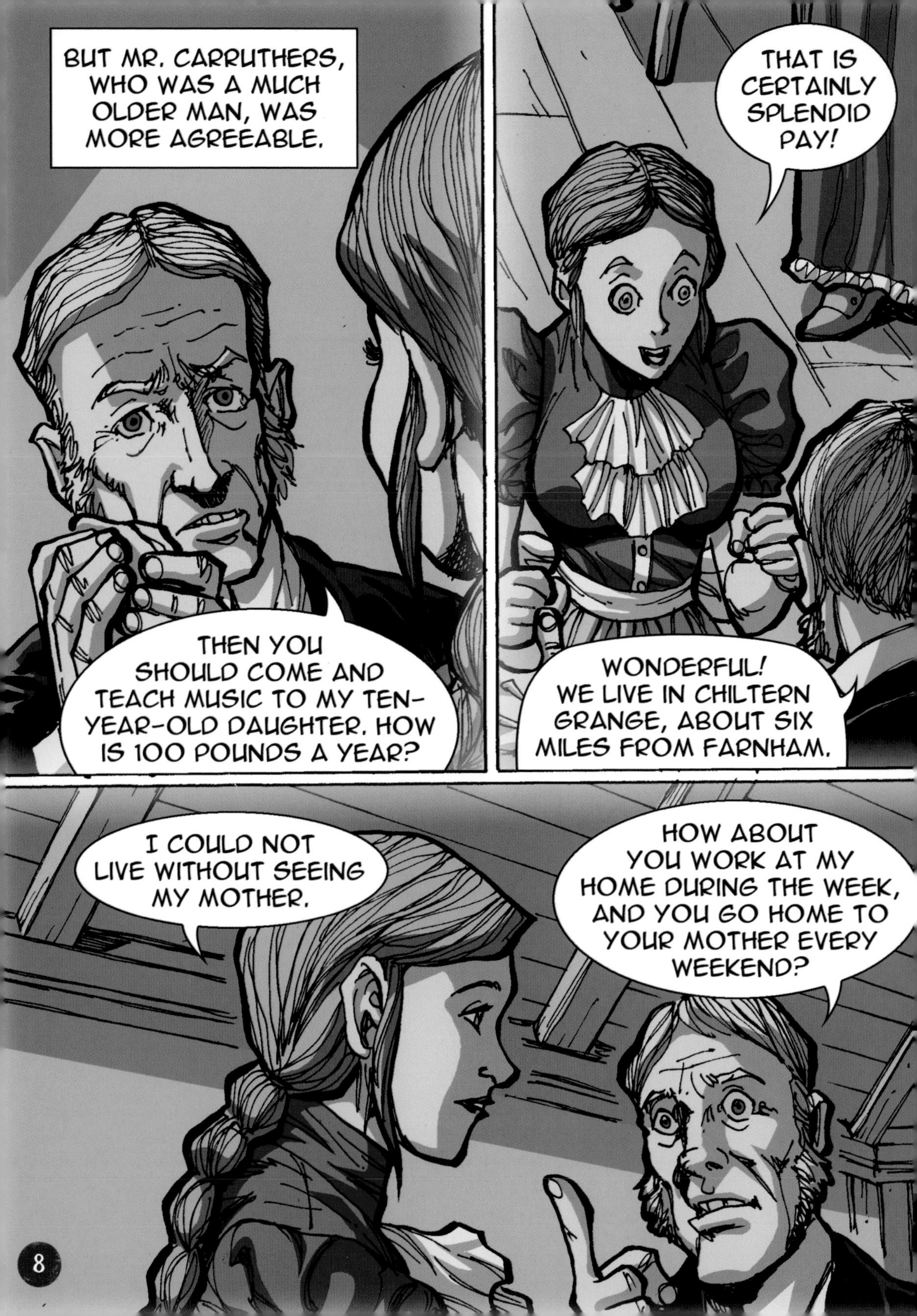
BUT MR. CARRUTHERS, WHO WAS A MUCH OLDER MAN, WAS MORE AGREEABLE.
THEN YOU SHOULD COME AND TEACH MUSIC TO MY TEN-YEAR-OLD DAUGHTER. HOW IS 100 POUNDS A YEAR?
THAT IS CERTAINLY SPLENDID PAY!
WONDERFUL! WE LIVE IN CHILTERN GRANGE, ABOUT SIX MILES FROM FARNHAM.
I COULD NOT LIVE WITHOUT SEEING MY MOTHER.
HOW ABOUT YOU WORK AT MY HOME DURING THE WEEK, AND YOU GO HOME TO YOUR MOTHER EVERY WEEKEND?

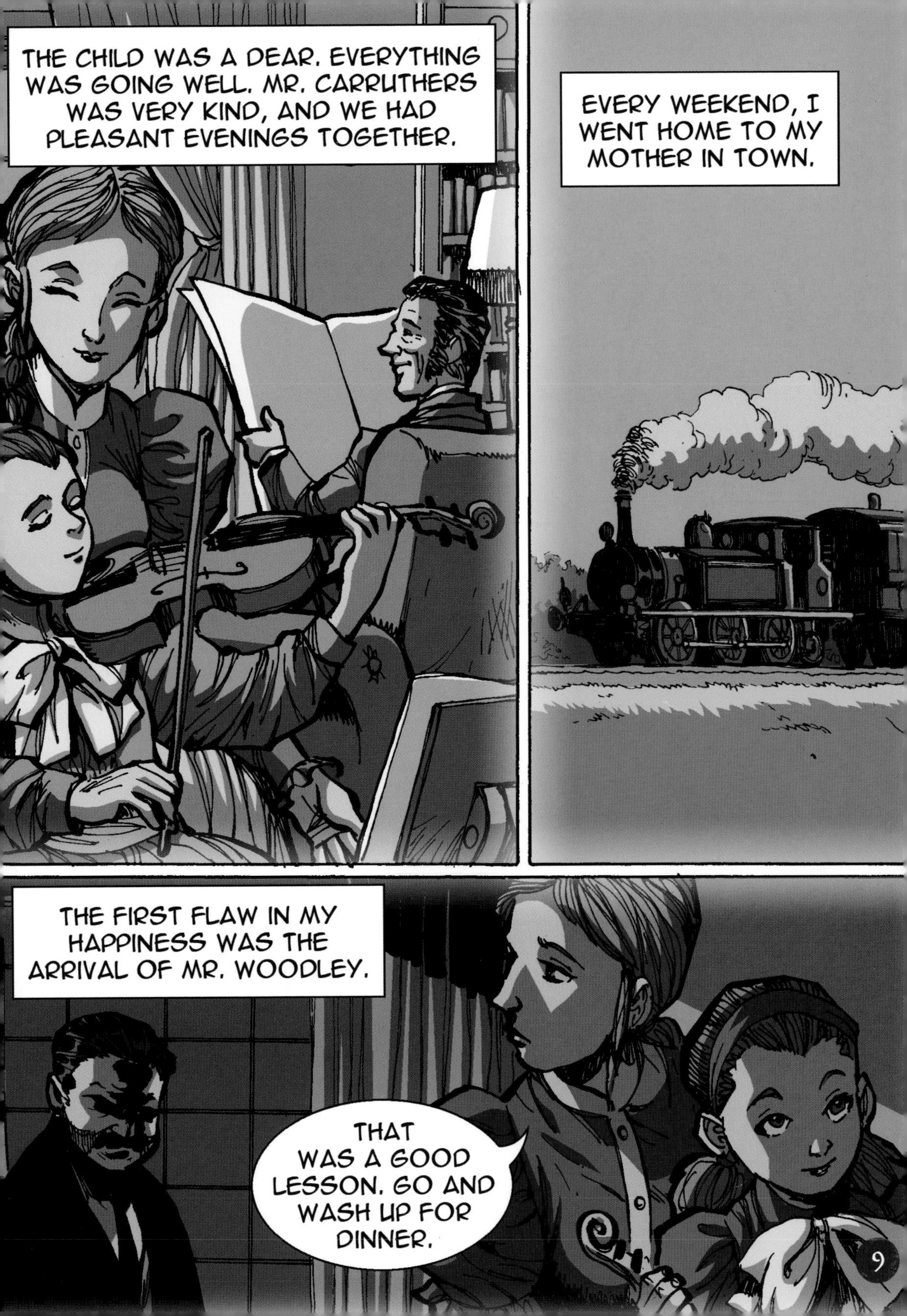
THE CHILD WAS A DEAR. EVERYTHING WAS GOING WELL. MR. CARRUTHERS WAS VERY KIND, AND WE HAD PLEASANT EVENINGS TOGETHER.
EVERY WEEKEND, I WENT HOME TO MY MOTHER IN TOWN.
THE FIRST FLAW IN MY HAPPINESS WAS THE ARRIVAL OF MR. WOODLEY.
THAT WAS A GOOD LESSON. GO AND WASH UP FOR DINNER.

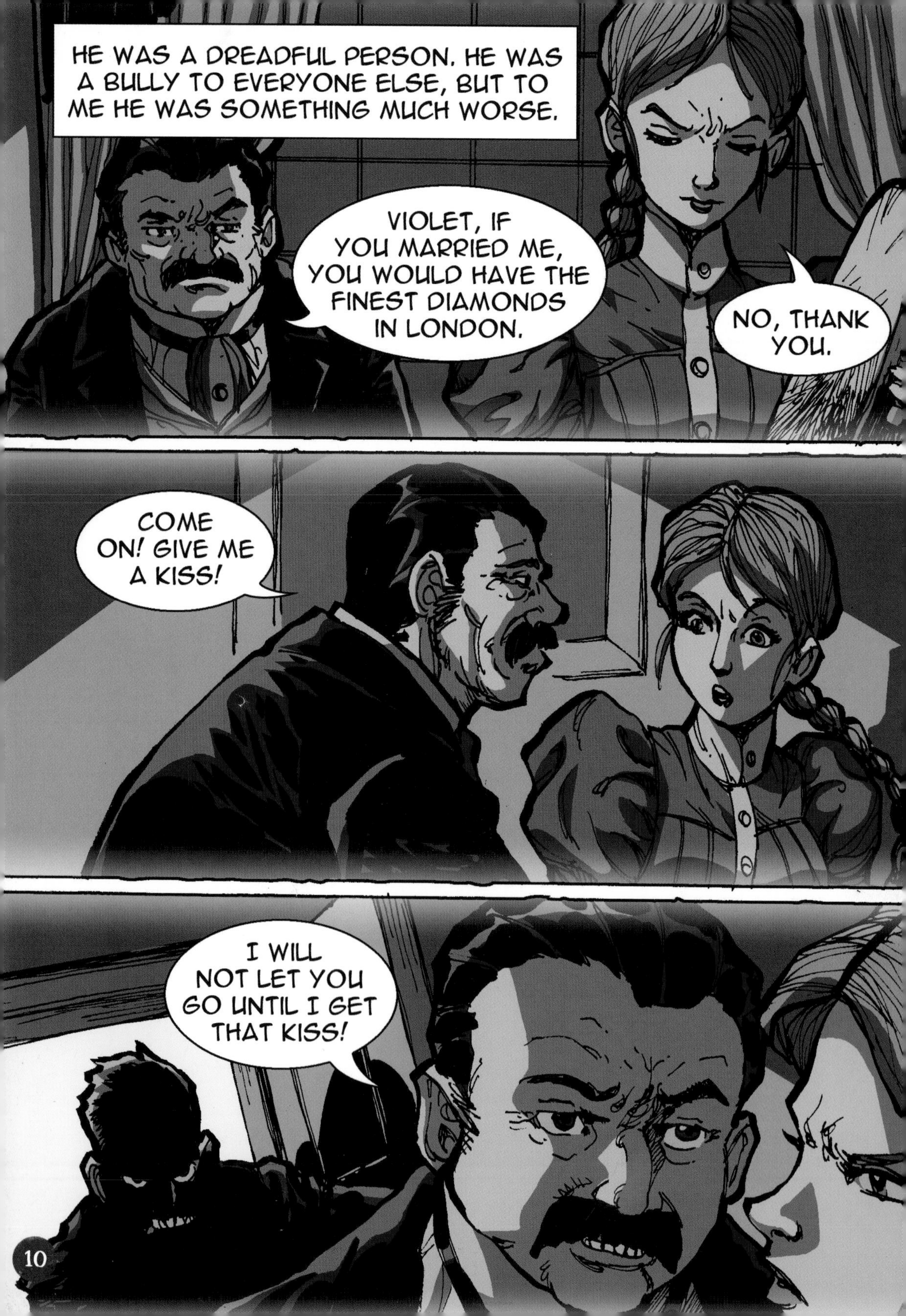
HE WAS A DREADFUL PERSON. HE WAS A BULLY TO EVERYONE ELSE, BUT TO ME HE WAS SOMETHING MUCH WORSE.
VIOLET, IF YOU MARRIED ME, YOU WOULD HAVE THE FINEST DIAMONDS IN LONDON.
NO, THANK YOU.
COME ON! GIVE ME A KISS!
I WILL NOT LET YOU GO UNTIL I GET THAT KISS!

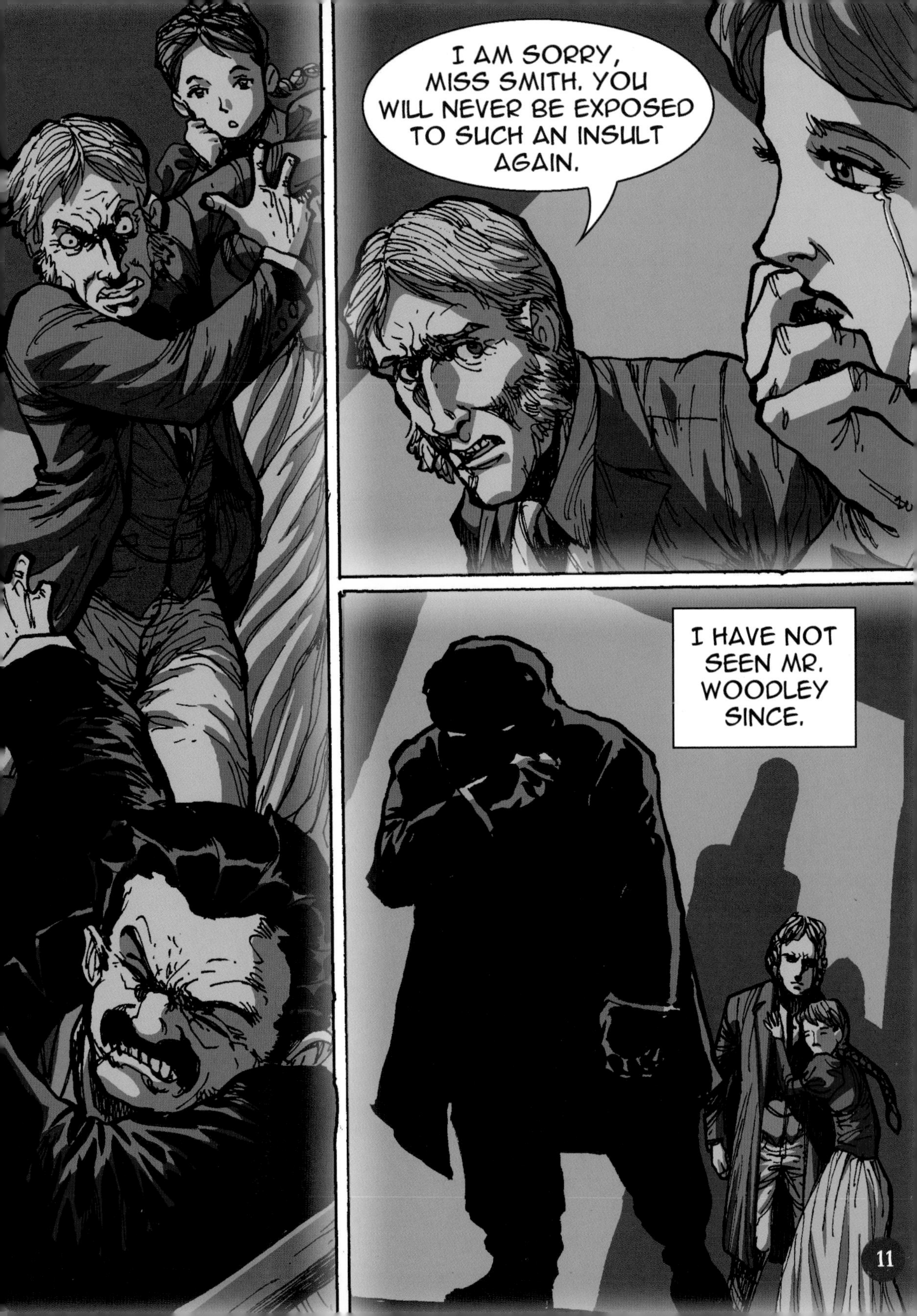
I AM SORRY, MISS SMITH. YOU WILL NEVER BE EXPOSED TO SUCH AN INSULT AGAIN.
I HAVE NOT SEEN MR. WOODLEY SINCE.

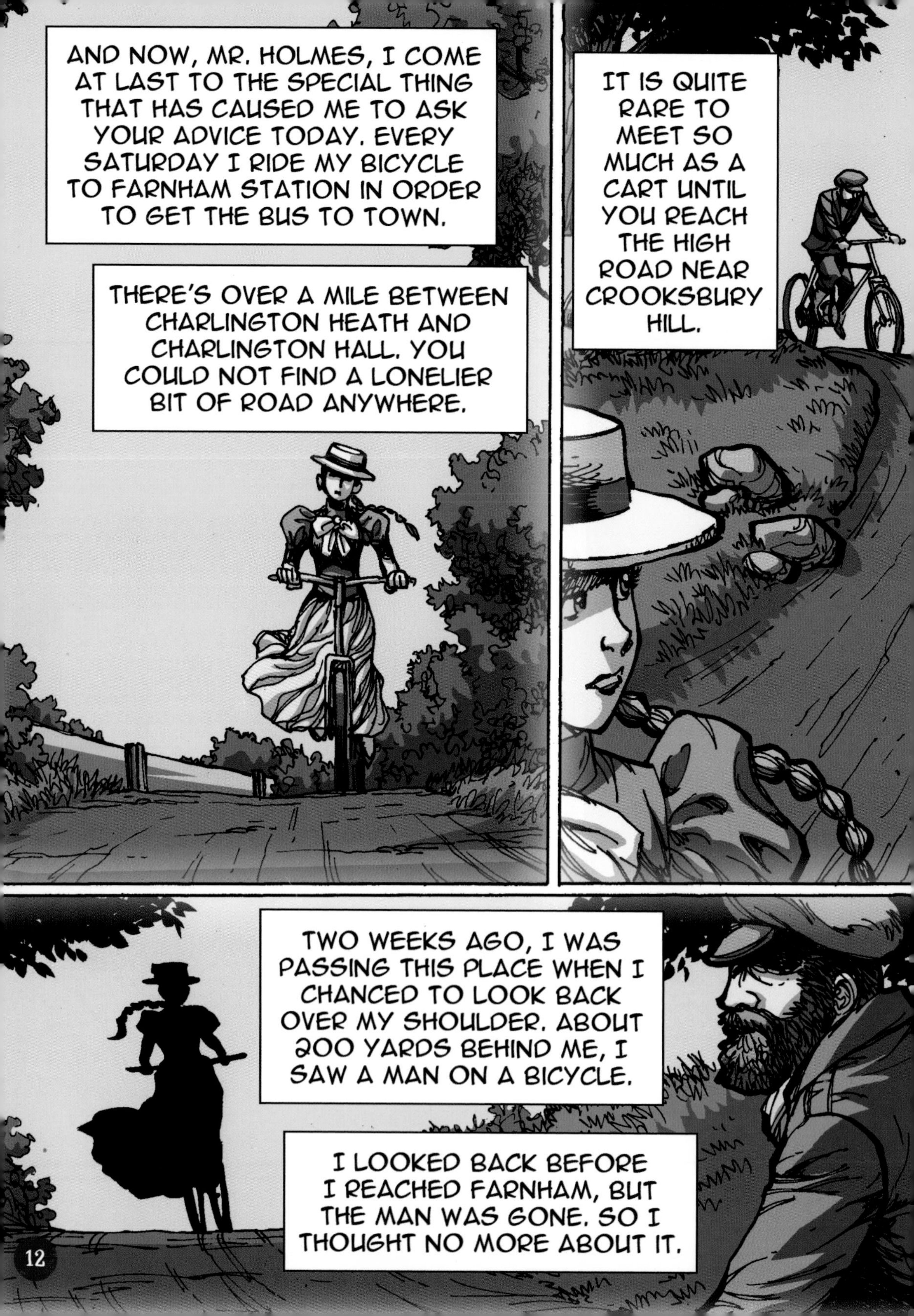
AND NOW, MR. HOLMES, I COME AT LAST TO THE SPECIAL THING THAT HAS CAUSED ME TO ASK YOUR ADVICE TODAY. EVERY SATURDAY I RIDE MY BICYCLE TO FARNHAM STATION IN ORDER TO GET THE BUS TO TOWN.
THERE'S OVER A MILE BETWEEN CHARLINGTON HEATH AND CHARLINGTON HALL. YOU COULD NOT FIND A LONELIER BIT OF ROAD ANYWHERE.
IT IS QUITE RARE TO MEET SO MUCH AS A CART UNTIL YOU REACH THE HIGH ROAD NEAR CROOKSBURY HILL.
TWO WEEKS AGO, I WAS PASSING THIS PLACE WHEN I CHANCED TO LOOK BACK OVER MY SHOULDER. ABOUT 200 YARDS BEHIND ME, I SAW A MAN ON A BICYCLE.
I LOOKED BACK BEFORE I REACHED FARNHAM, BUT THE MAN WAS GONE. SO I THOUGHT NO MORE ABOUT IT.

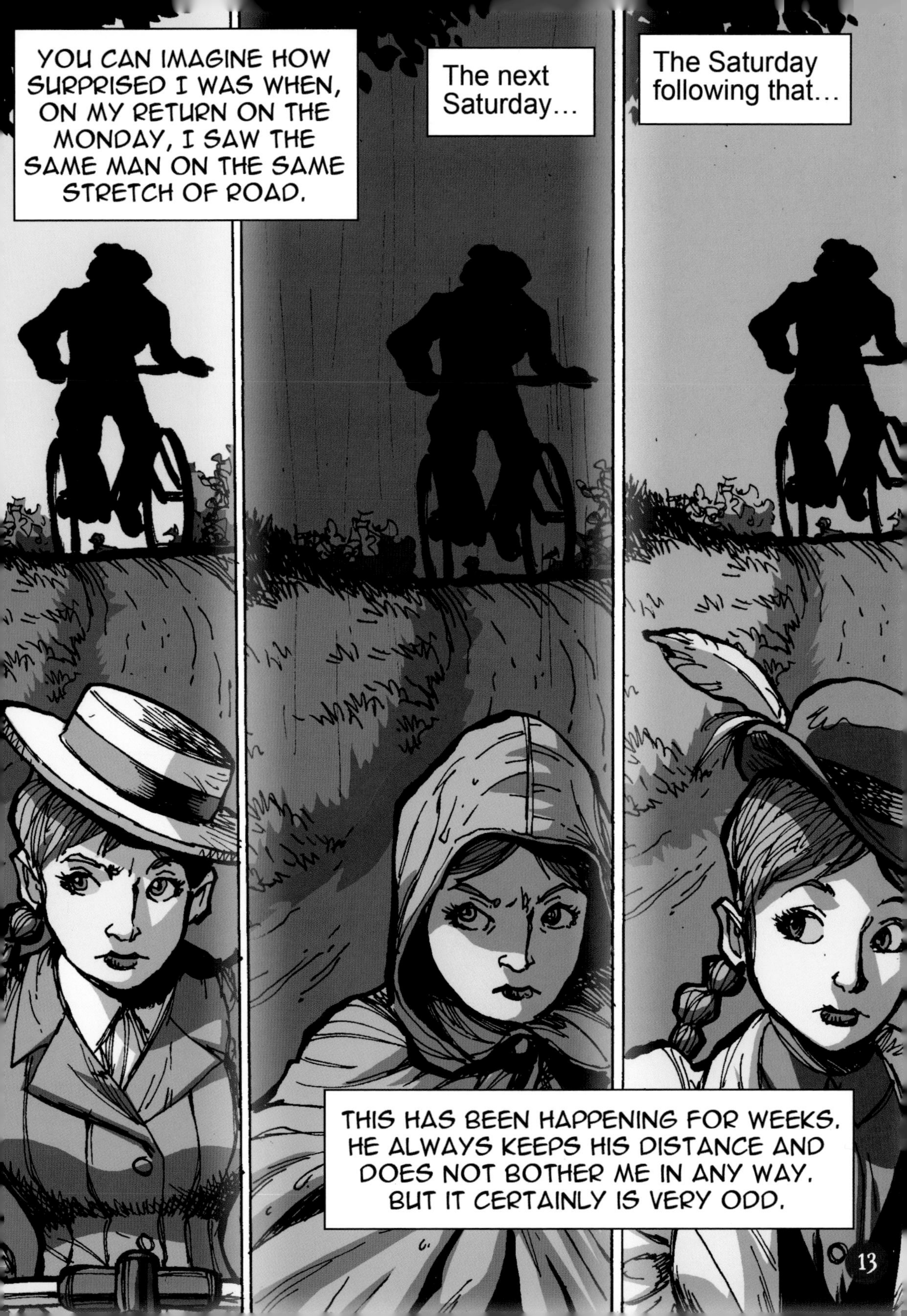
YOU CAN IMAGINE HOW SURPRISED I WAS WHEN, ON MY RETURN ON THE MONDAY, I SAW THE SAME MAN ON THE SAME STRETCH OF ROAD.
The next Saturday…
The Saturday following that…
THIS HAS BEEN HAPPENING FOR WEEKS. HE ALWAYS KEEPS HIS DISTANCE AND DOES NOT BOTHER ME IN ANY WAY. BUT IT CERTAINLY IS VERY ODD.

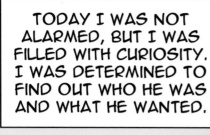

TODAY I WAS NOT ALARMED, BUT I WAS FILLED WITH CURIOSITY. I WAS DETERMINED TO FIND OUT WHO HE WAS AND WHAT HE WANTED.

I LAID A TRAP FOR HIM. I PEDALED QUICKLY AROUND A SHARP TURN.

I EXPECTED HIM TO SHOOT ROUND AND PASS ME BEFORE HE COULD STOP.

BUT HE NEVER APPEARED.

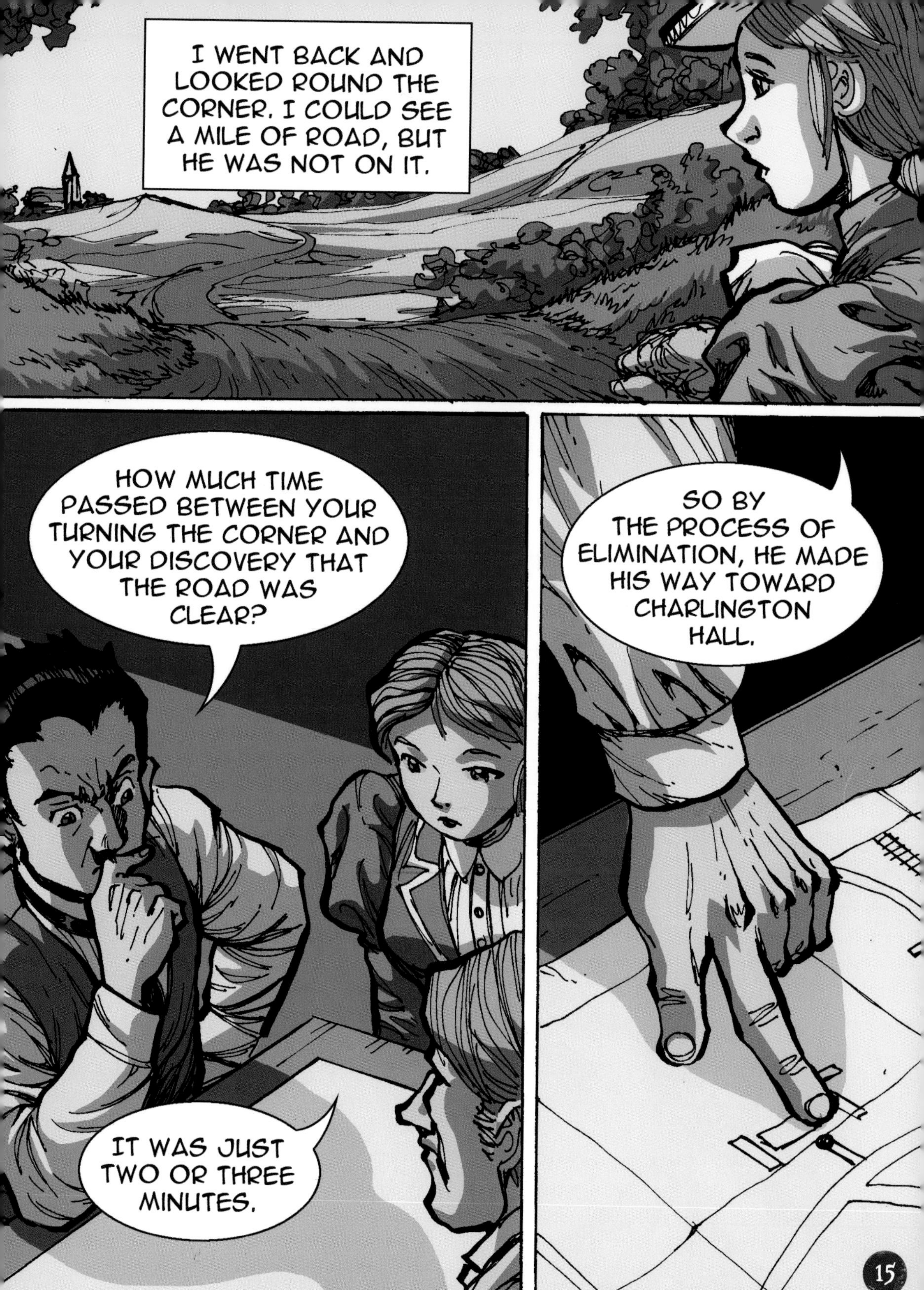
I WENT BACK AND LOOKED ROUND THE CORNER. I COULD SEE A MILE OF ROAD, BUT HE WAS NOT ON IT.
HOW MUCH TIME PASSED BETWEEN YOUR TURNING THE CORNER AND YOUR DISCOVERY THAT THE ROAD WAS CLEAR?
IT WAS JUST TWO OR THREE MINUTES.
SO BY THE PROCESS OF ELIMINATION, HE MADE HIS WAY TOWARD CHARLINGTON HALL.

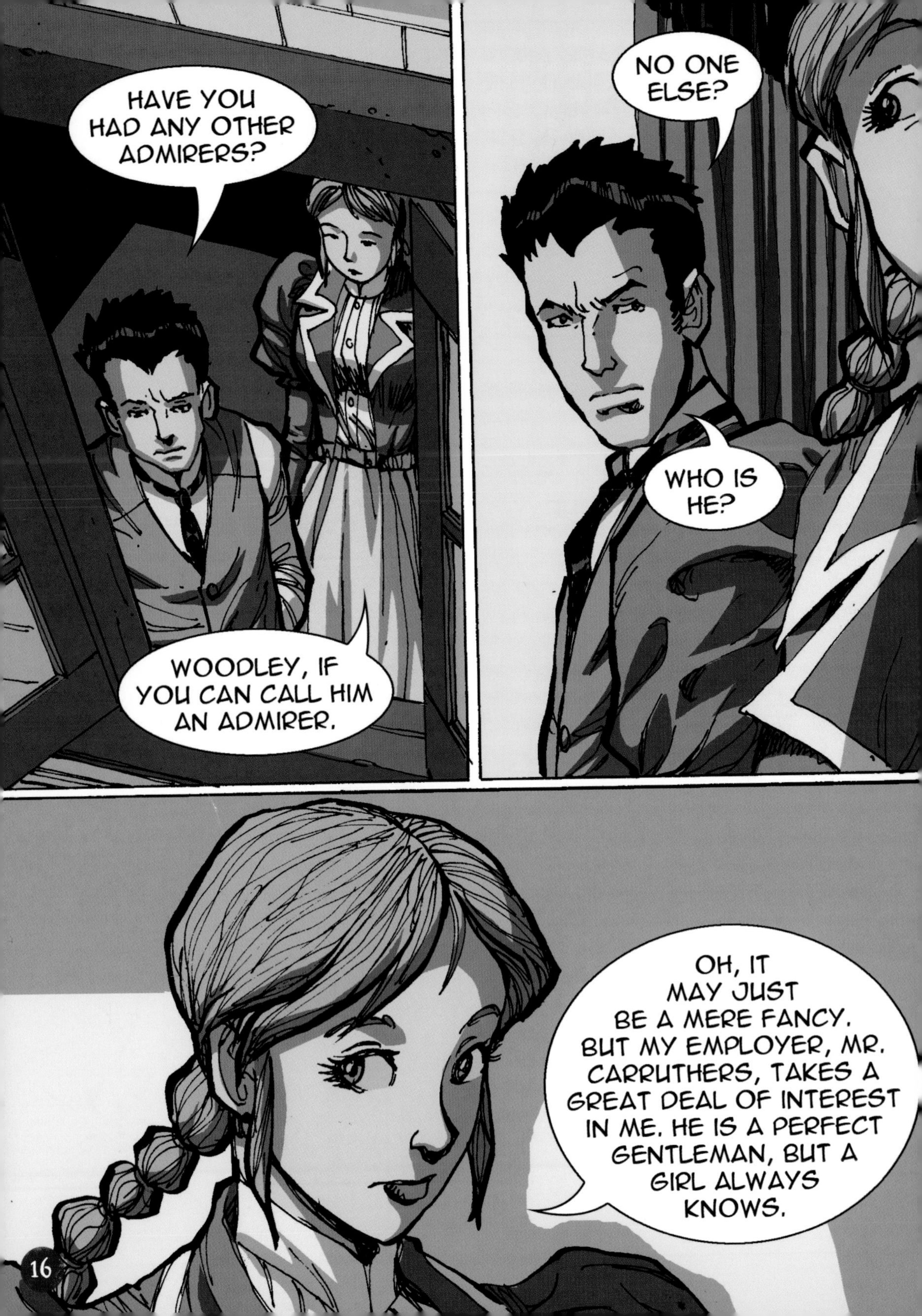
HAVE YOU HAD ANY OTHER ADMIRERS?
WOODLEY, IF YOU CAN CALL HIM AN ADMIRER.
NO ONE ELSE?
WHO IS HE?
OH, IT MAY JUST BE A MERE FANCY. BUT MY EMPLOYER, MR. CARRUTHERS, TAKES A GREAT DEAL OF INTEREST IN ME. HE IS A PERFECT GENTLEMAN, BUT A GIRL ALWAYS KNOWS.

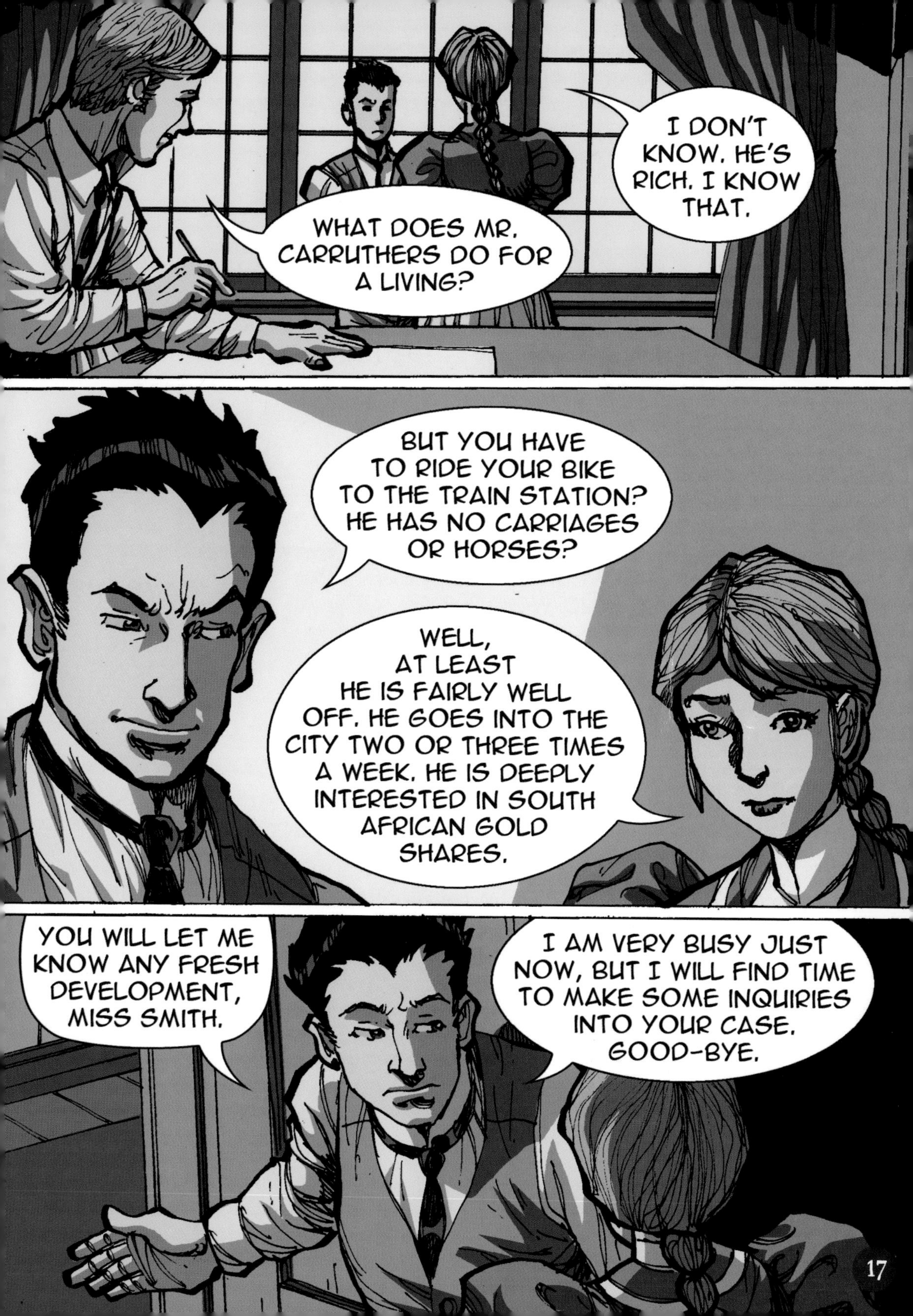
WHAT DOES MR. CARRUTHERS DO FOR A LIVING?
I DON'T KNOW. HE'S RICH. I KNOW THAT.
BUT YOU HAVE TO RIDE YOUR BIKE TO THE TRAIN STATION? HE HAS NO CARRIAGES OR HORSES?
WELL, AT LEAST HE IS FAIRLY WELL OFF. HE GOES INTO THE CITY TWO OR THREE TIMES A WEEK. HE IS DEEPLY INTERESTED IN SOUTH AFRICAN GOLD SHARES.
YOU WILL LET ME KNOW ANY FRESH DEVELOPMENT, MISS SMITH.
I AM VERY BUSY JUST NOW, BUT I WILL FIND TIME TO MAKE SOME INQUIRIES INTO YOUR CASE. GOOD-BYE.

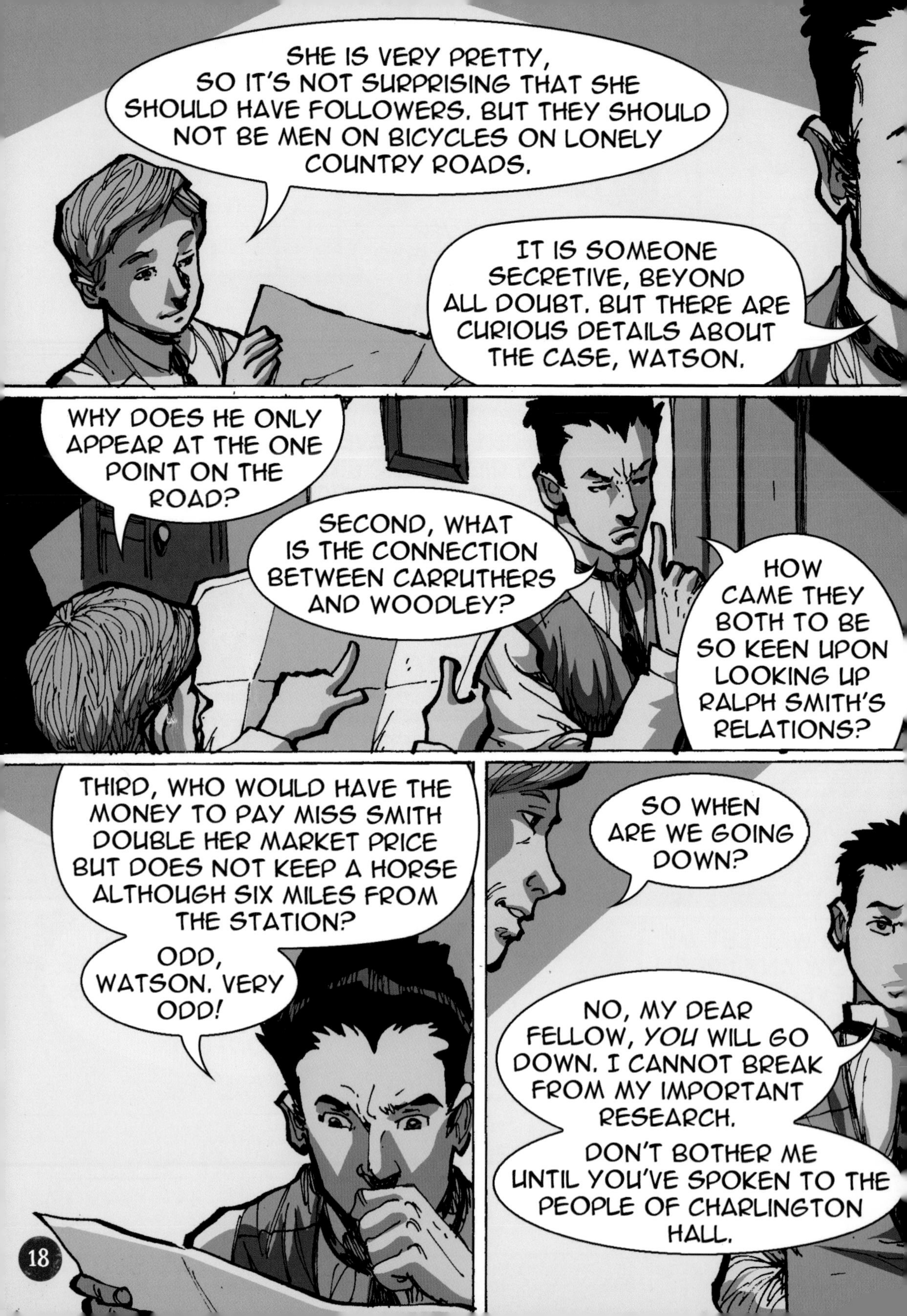
SHE IS VERY PRETTY, SO IT'S NOT SURPRISING THAT SHE SHOULD HAVE FOLLOWERS. BUT THEY SHOULD NOT BE MEN ON BICYCLES ON LONELY COUNTRY ROADS.
IT IS SOMEONE SECRETIVE, BEYOND ALL DOUBT. BUT THERE ARE CURIOUS DETAILS ABOUT THE CASE, WATSON.
WHY DOES HE ONLY APPEAR AT THE ONE POINT ON THE ROAD?
SECOND, WHAT IS THE CONNECTION BETWEEN CARRUTHERS AND WOODLEY?
HOW CAME THEY BOTH TO BE SO KEEN UPON LOOKING UP RALPH SMITH'S RELATIONS?
THIRD, WHO WOULD HAVE THE MONEY TO PAY MISS SMITH DOUBLE HER MARKET PRICE BUT DOES NOT KEEP A HORSE ALTHOUGH SIX MILES FROM THE STATION?
ODD, WATSON. VERY ODD!
SO WHEN ARE WE GOING DOWN?
NO, MY DEAR FELLOW, *YOU* WILL GO DOWN. I CANNOT BREAK FROM MY IMPORTANT RESEARCH.
DON'T BOTHER ME UNTIL YOU'VE SPOKEN TO THE PEOPLE OF CHARLINGTON HALL.

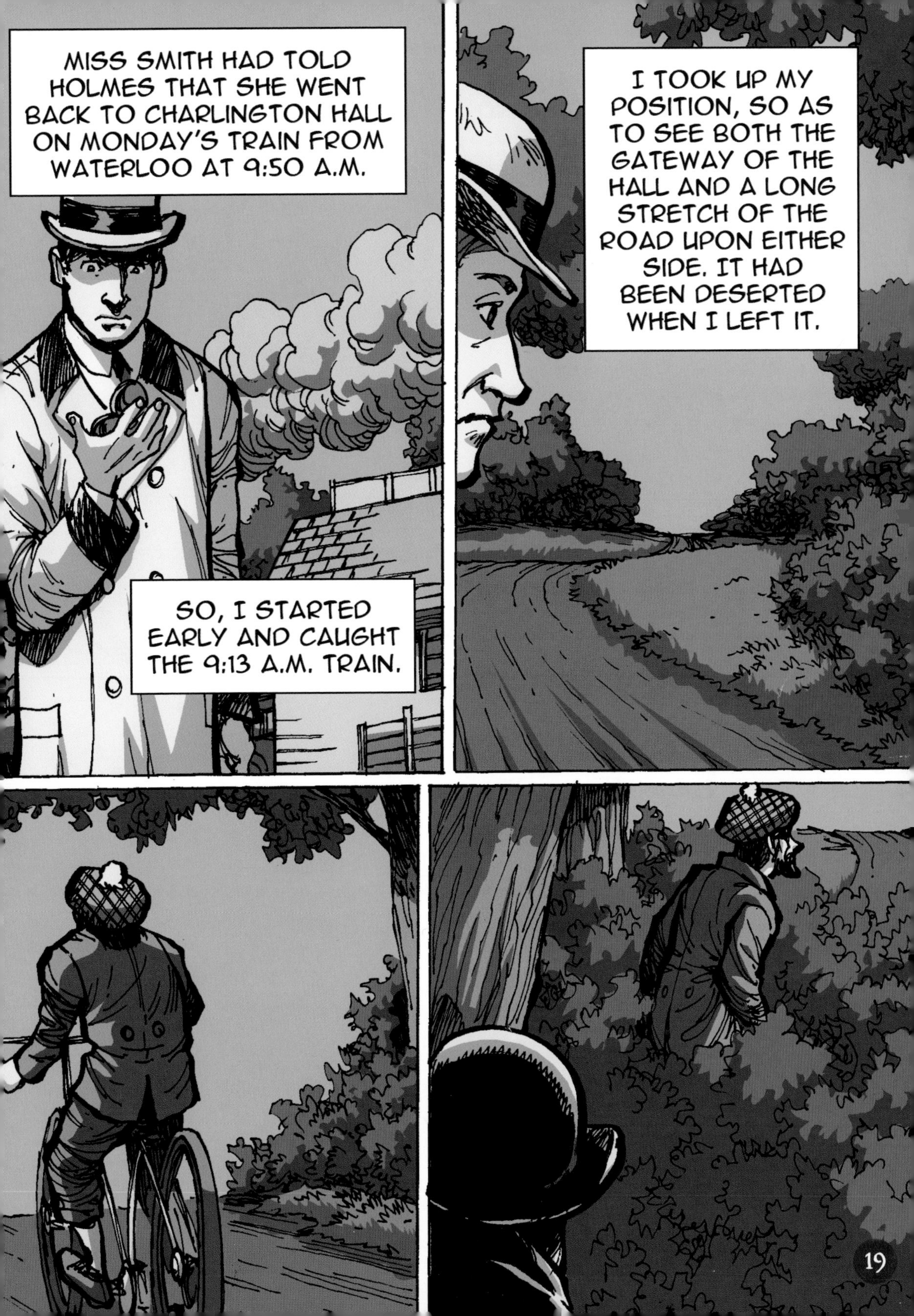
MISS SMITH HAD TOLD HOLMES THAT SHE WENT BACK TO CHARLINGTON HALL ON MONDAY'S TRAIN FROM WATERLOO AT 9:50 A.M.
SO, I STARTED EARLY AND CAUGHT THE 9:13 A.M. TRAIN.
I TOOK UP MY POSITION, SO AS TO SEE BOTH THE GATEWAY OF THE HALL AND A LONG STRETCH OF THE ROAD UPON EITHER SIDE. IT HAD BEEN DESERTED WHEN I LEFT IT.

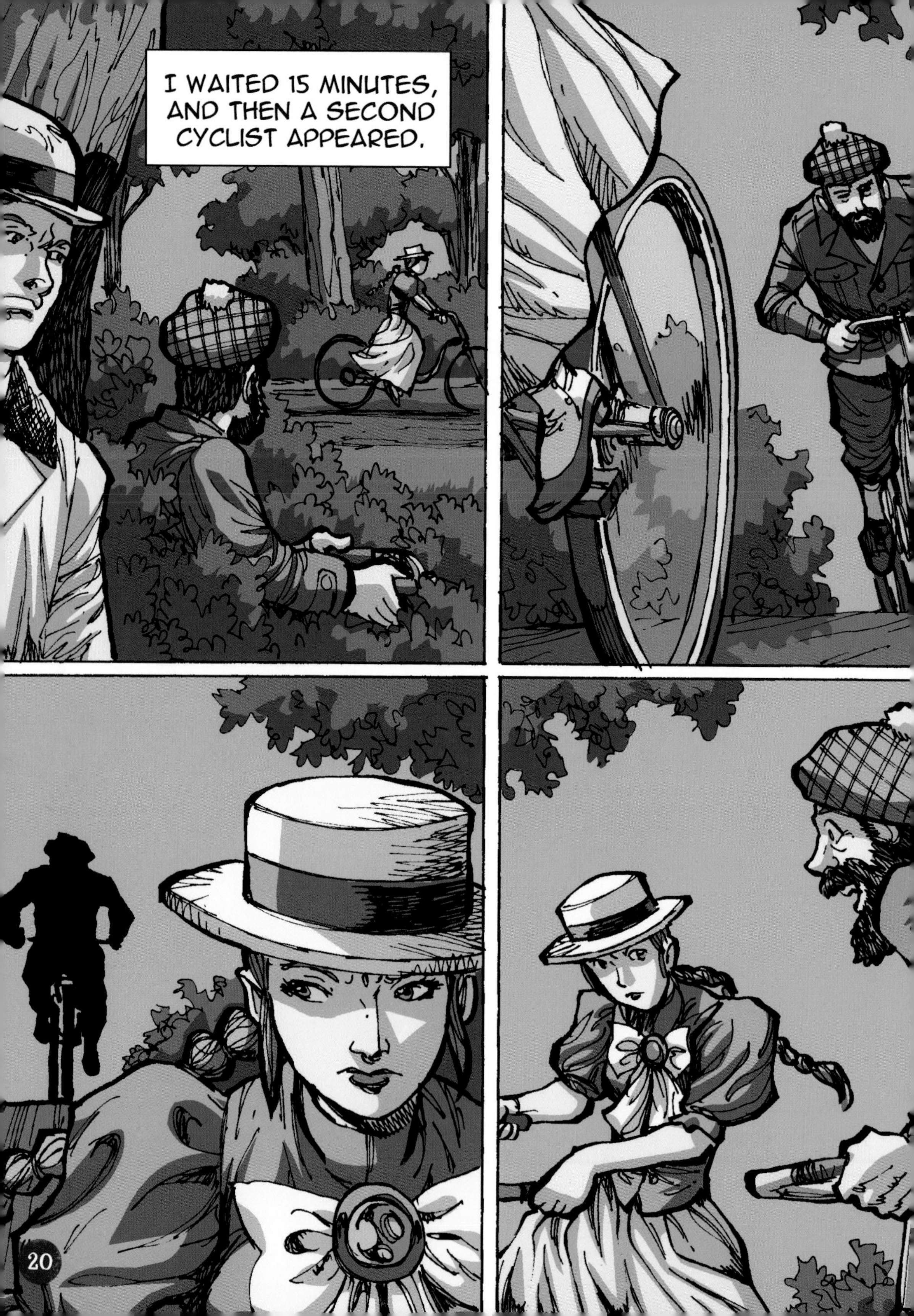
I WAITED 15 MINUTES, AND THEN A SECOND CYCLIST APPEARED.

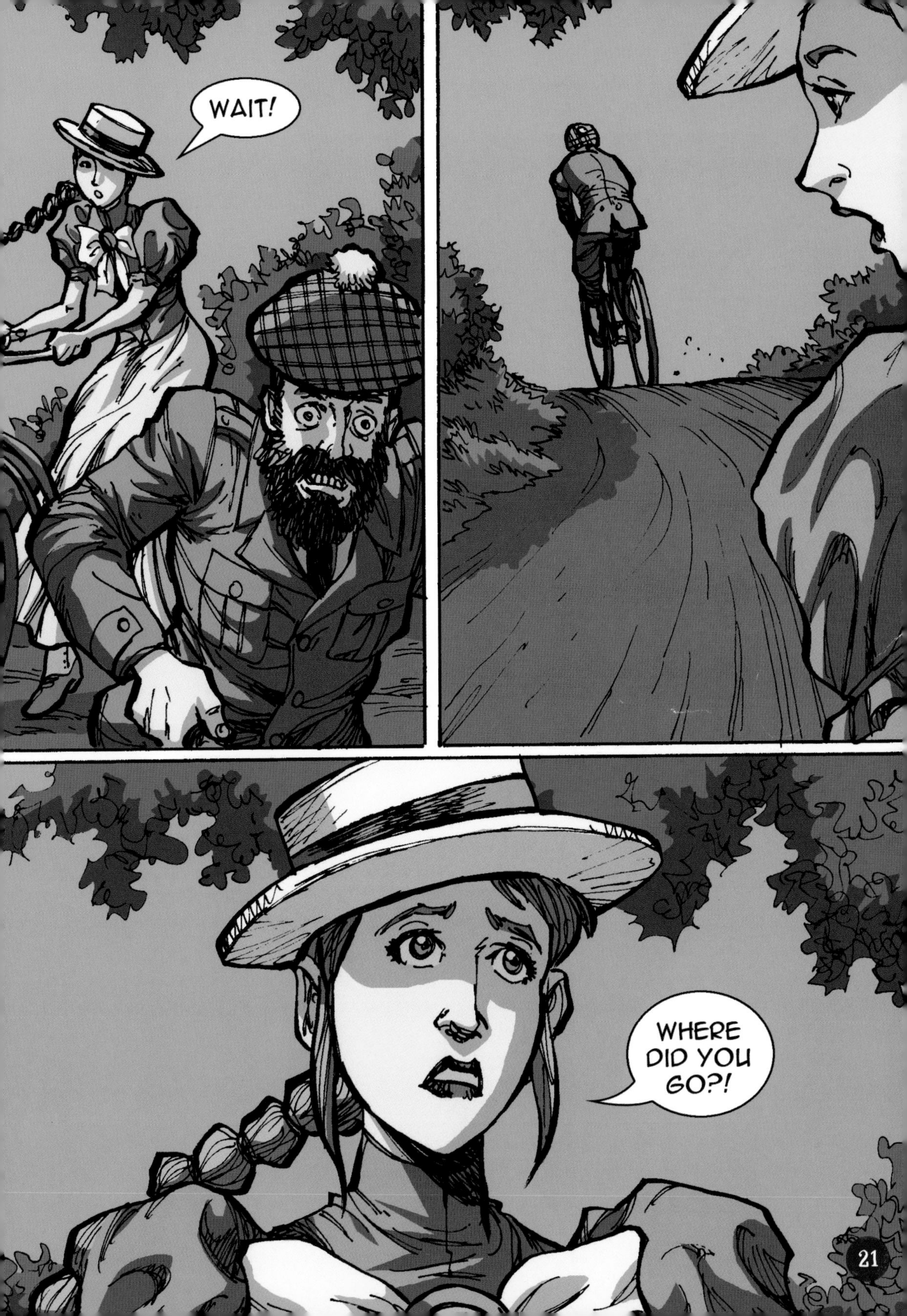
WAIT!
WHERE DID YOU GO?!

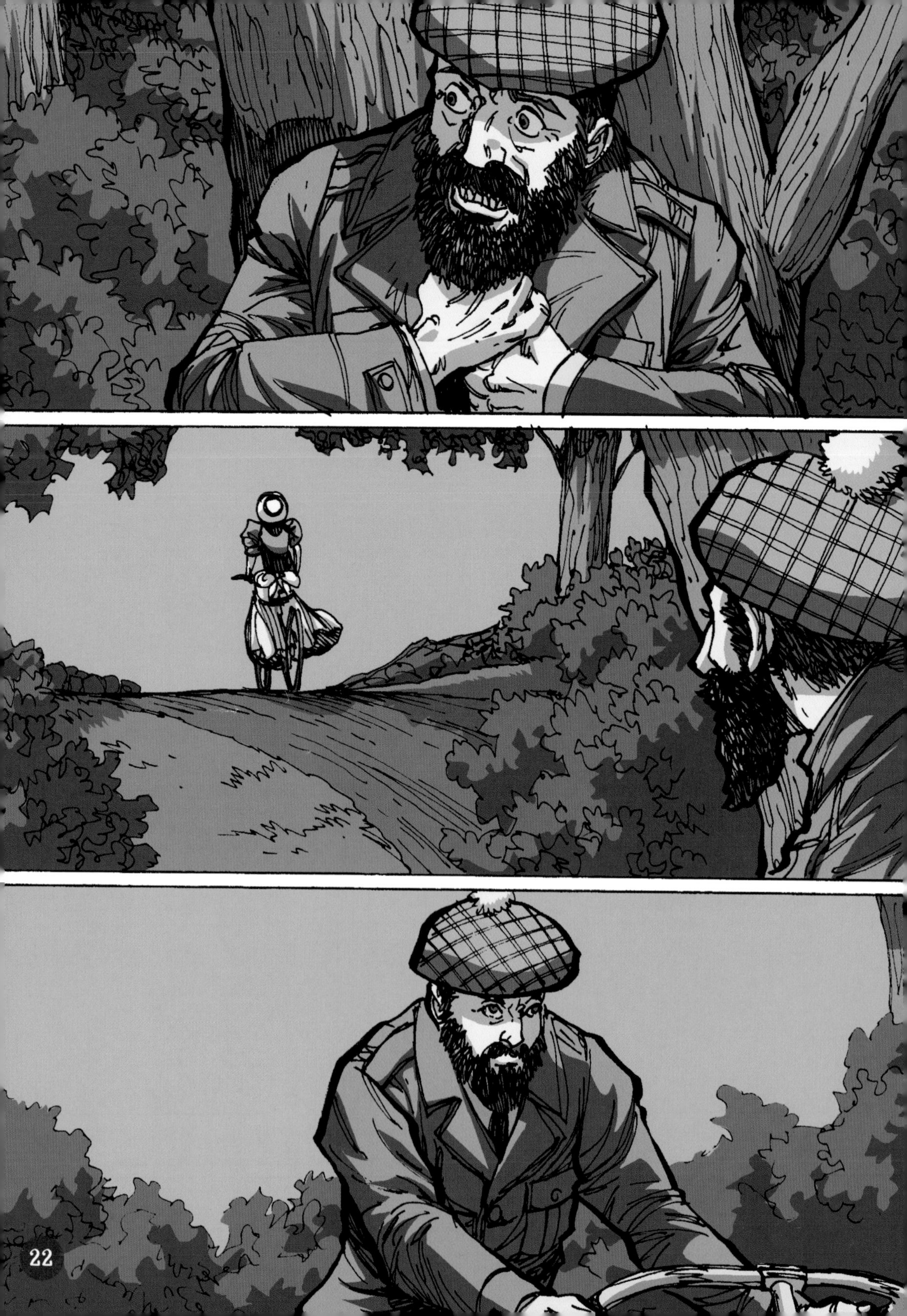

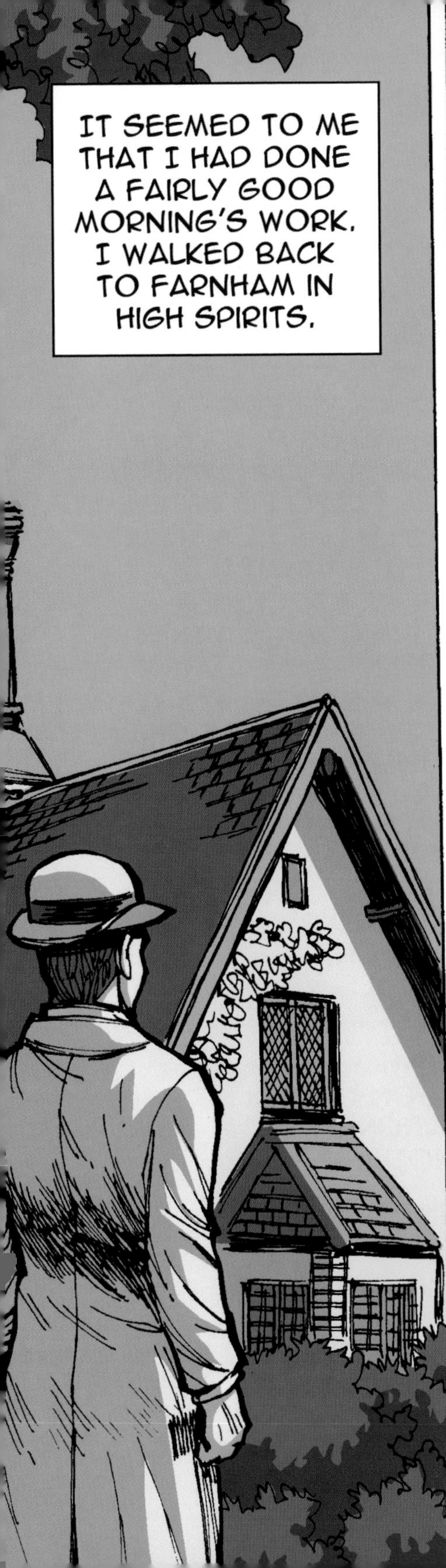
IT SEEMED TO ME THAT I HAD DONE A FAIRLY GOOD MORNING'S WORK. I WALKED BACK TO FARNHAM IN HIGH SPIRITS.

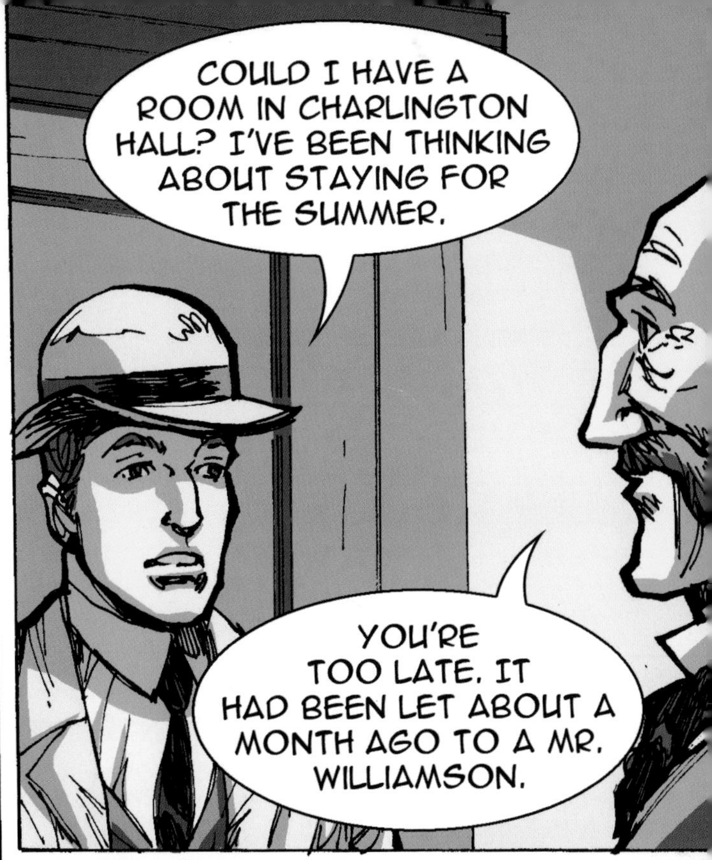
COULD I HAVE A ROOM IN CHARLINGTON HALL? I'VE BEEN THINKING ABOUT STAYING FOR THE SUMMER.
YOU'RE TOO LATE. IT HAD BEEN LET ABOUT A MONTH AGO TO A MR. WILLIAMSON.

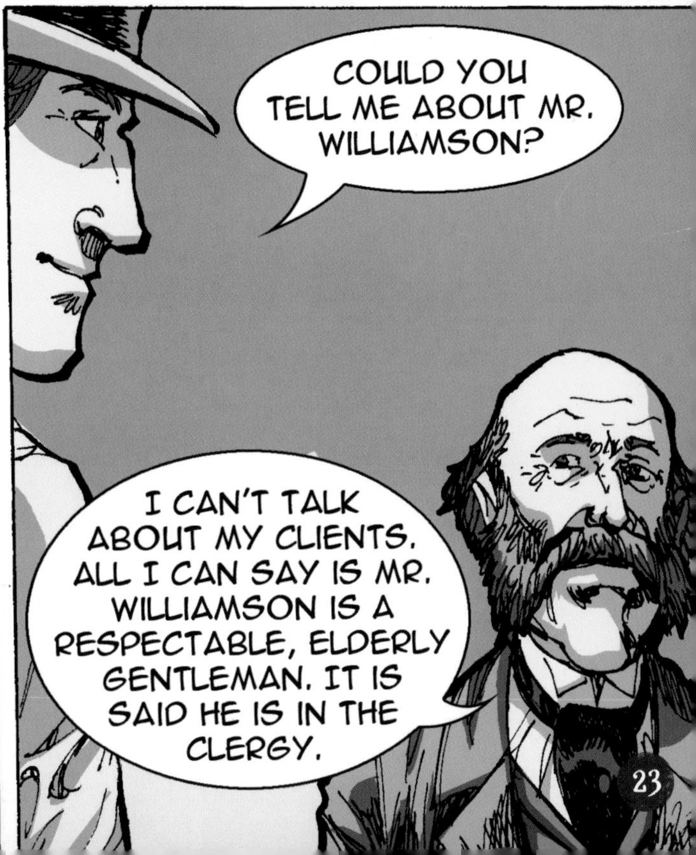
COULD YOU TELL ME ABOUT MR. WILLIAMSON?
I CAN'T TALK ABOUT MY CLIENTS. ALL I CAN SAY IS MR. WILLIAMSON IS A RESPECTABLE, ELDERLY GENTLEMAN. IT IS SAID HE IS IN THE CLERGY.

HOLMES LISTENED TO THE LONG REPORT I PRESENTED TO HIM THAT EVENING. IT DID NOT GET THE PRAISE I HAD HOPED FOR.

YOUR HIDING PLACE, MY DEAR WATSON, WAS VERY FAULTY. YOU CAN TELL ME EVEN LESS THAN MISS SMITH!

SHE THINKS SHE DOES NOT KNOW THE MAN, BUT I AM SURE SHE DOES. WHY ELSE WOULD HE BE SO CAREFUL THAT SHE NOT SEE HIS FEATURES?

YOU REALLY HAVE DONE REMARKABLY BADLY.

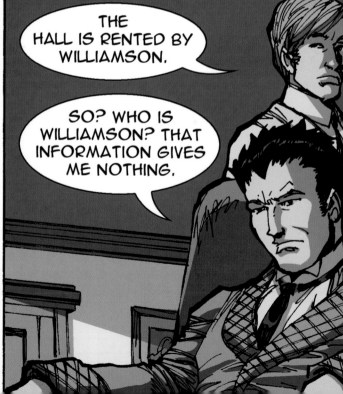

THE HALL IS RENTED BY WILLIAMSON.

SO? WHO IS WILLIAMSON? THAT INFORMATION GIVES ME NOTHING.

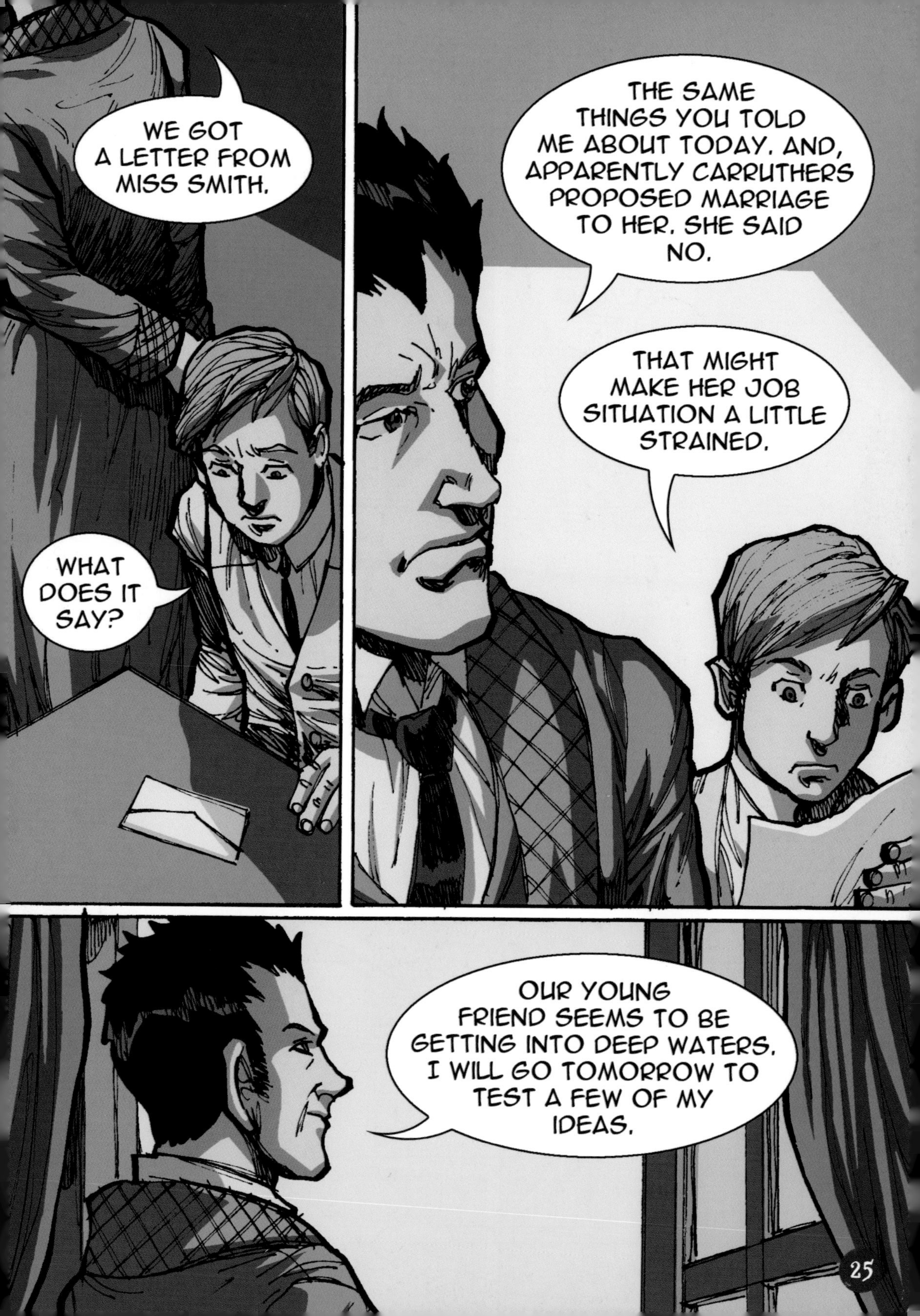
WE GOT A LETTER FROM MISS SMITH.
WHAT DOES IT SAY?
THE SAME THINGS YOU TOLD ME ABOUT TODAY. AND, APPARENTLY CARRUTHERS PROPOSED MARRIAGE TO HER. SHE SAID NO.
THAT MIGHT MAKE HER JOB SITUATION A LITTLE STRAINED.
OUR YOUNG FRIEND SEEMS TO BE GETTING INTO DEEP WATERS. I WILL GO TOMORROW TO TEST A FEW OF MY IDEAS.

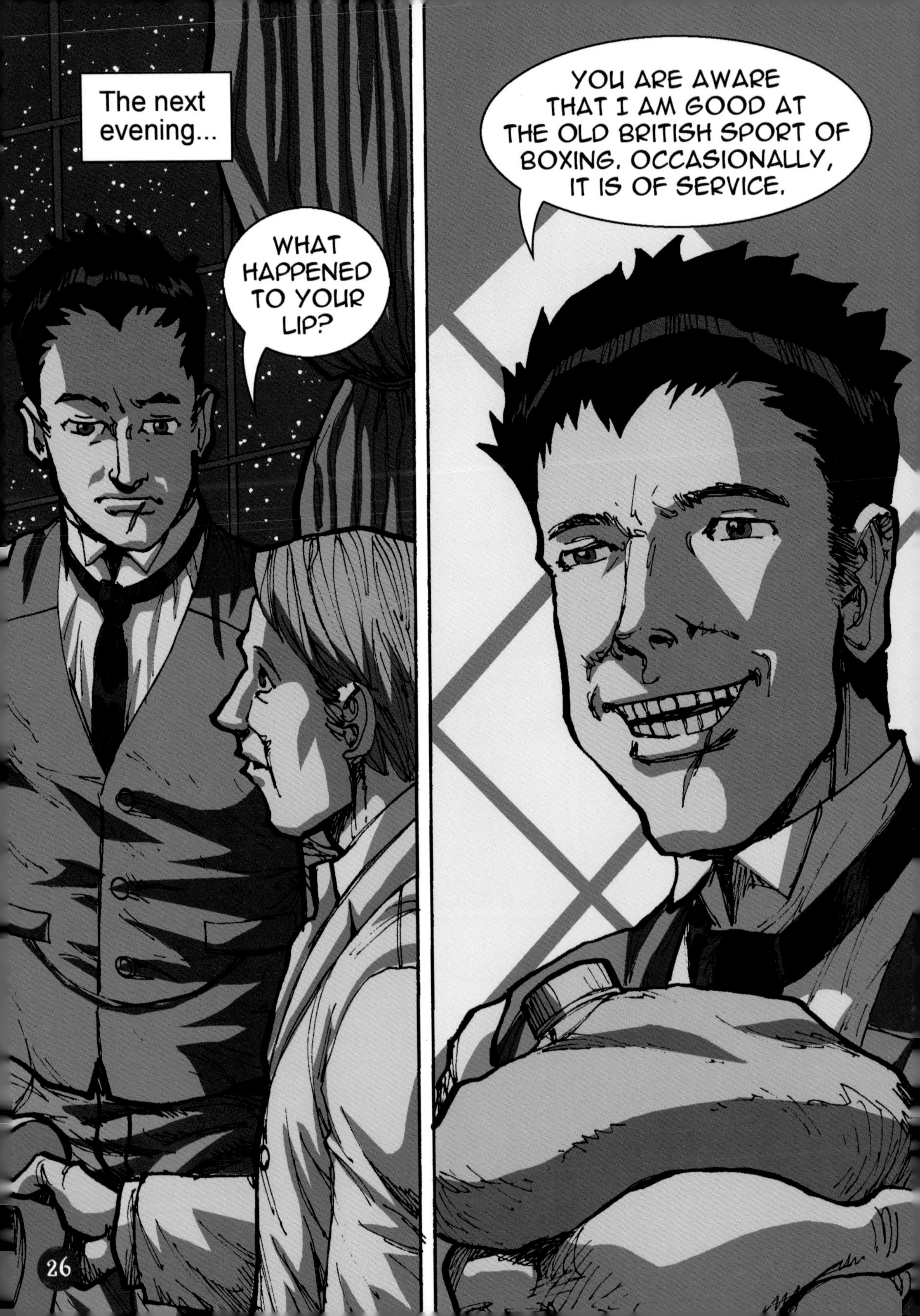
The next evening...
WHAT HAPPENED TO YOUR LIP?
YOU ARE AWARE THAT I AM GOOD AT THE OLD BRITISH SPORT OF BOXING. OCCASIONALLY, IT IS OF SERVICE.

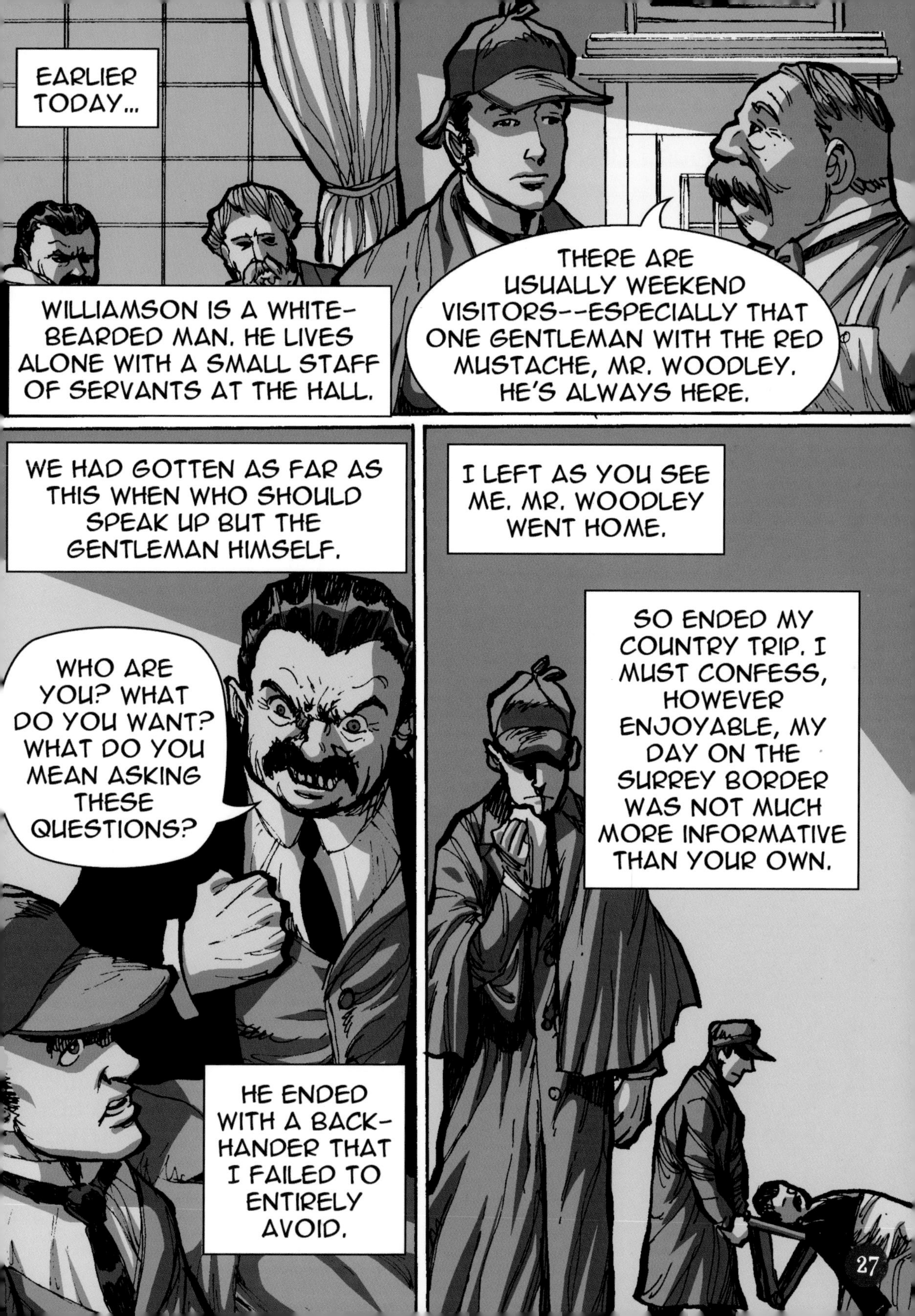
EARLIER TODAY...
WILLIAMSON IS A WHITE-BEARDED MAN. HE LIVES ALONE WITH A SMALL STAFF OF SERVANTS AT THE HALL.
THERE ARE USUALLY WEEKEND VISITORS--ESPECIALLY THAT ONE GENTLEMAN WITH THE RED MUSTACHE, MR. WOODLEY. HE'S ALWAYS HERE.
WE HAD GOTTEN AS FAR AS THIS WHEN WHO SHOULD SPEAK UP BUT THE GENTLEMAN HIMSELF.
WHO ARE YOU? WHAT DO YOU WANT? WHAT DO YOU MEAN ASKING THESE QUESTIONS?
HE ENDED WITH A BACK-HANDER THAT I FAILED TO ENTIRELY AVOID.
I LEFT AS YOU SEE ME. MR. WOODLEY WENT HOME.
SO ENDED MY COUNTRY TRIP. I MUST CONFESS, HOWEVER ENJOYABLE, MY DAY ON THE SURREY BORDER WAS NOT MUCH MORE INFORMATIVE THAN YOUR OWN.

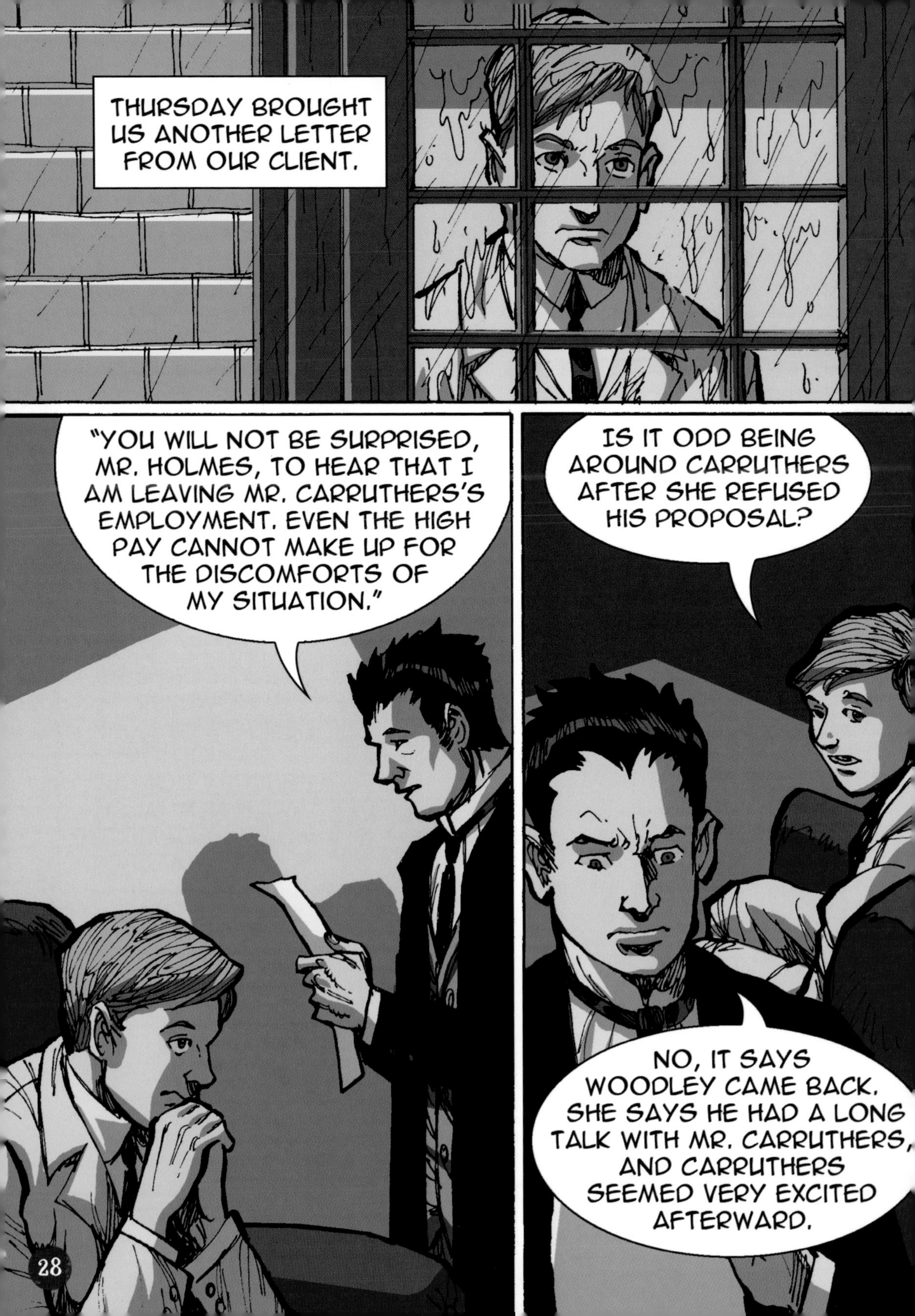
THURSDAY BROUGHT US ANOTHER LETTER FROM OUR CLIENT.
"YOU WILL NOT BE SURPRISED, MR. HOLMES, TO HEAR THAT I AM LEAVING MR. CARRUTHERS'S EMPLOYMENT. EVEN THE HIGH PAY CANNOT MAKE UP FOR THE DISCOMFORTS OF MY SITUATION."
IS IT ODD BEING AROUND CARRUTHERS AFTER SHE REFUSED HIS PROPOSAL?
NO, IT SAYS WOODLEY CAME BACK. SHE SAYS HE HAD A LONG TALK WITH MR. CARRUTHERS, AND CARRUTHERS SEEMED VERY EXCITED AFTERWARD.

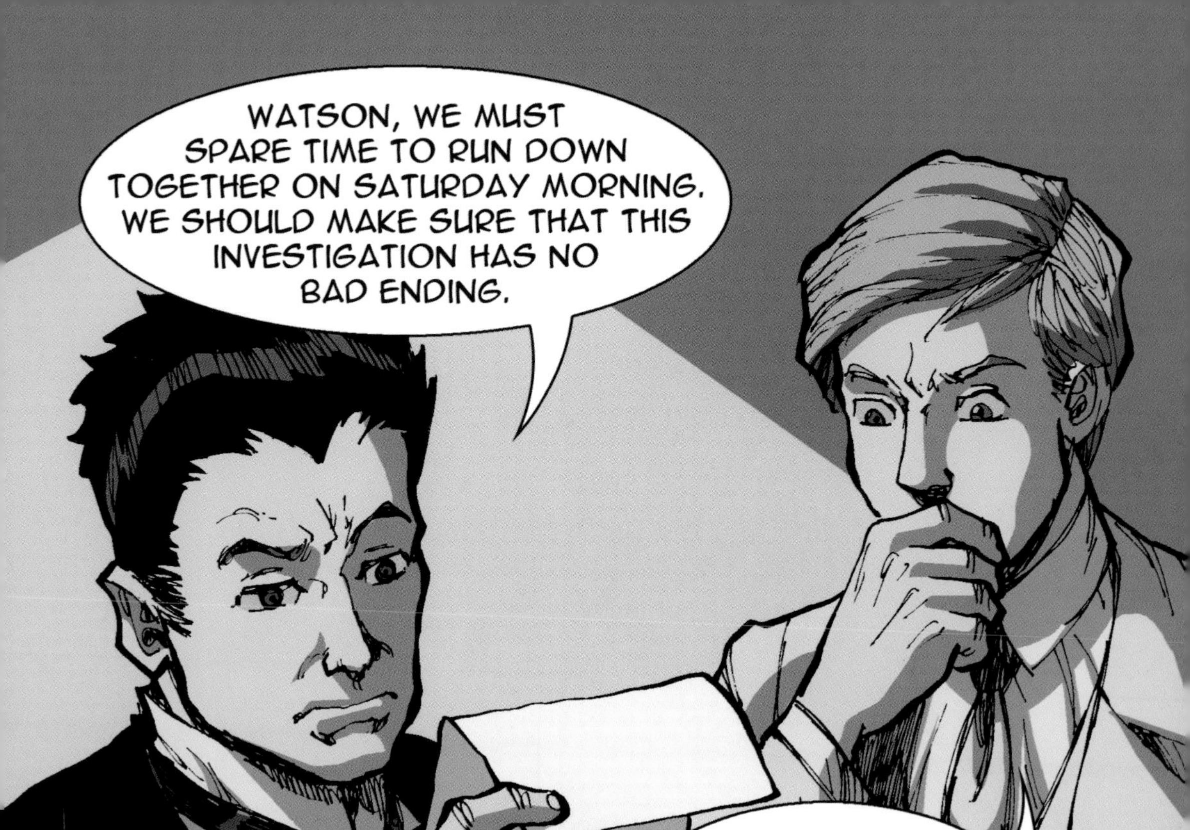
WATSON, WE MUST SPARE TIME TO RUN DOWN TOGETHER ON SATURDAY MORNING. WE SHOULD MAKE SURE THAT THIS INVESTIGATION HAS NO BAD ENDING.
I ADMIT I HAVE NOT TAKEN A VERY SERIOUS VIEW OF THE CASE. TO ME, IT SEEMS MORE BIZARRE THAN DANGEROUS.

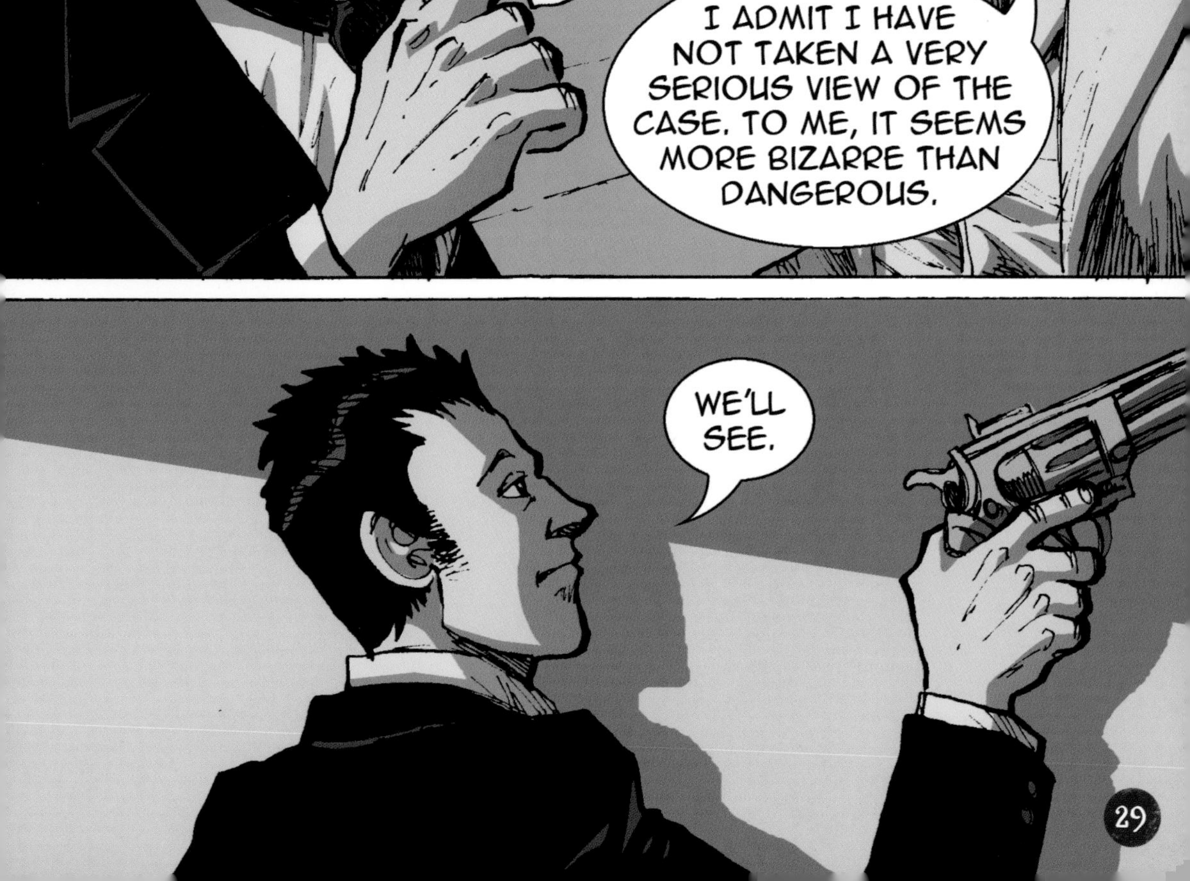
WE'LL SEE.

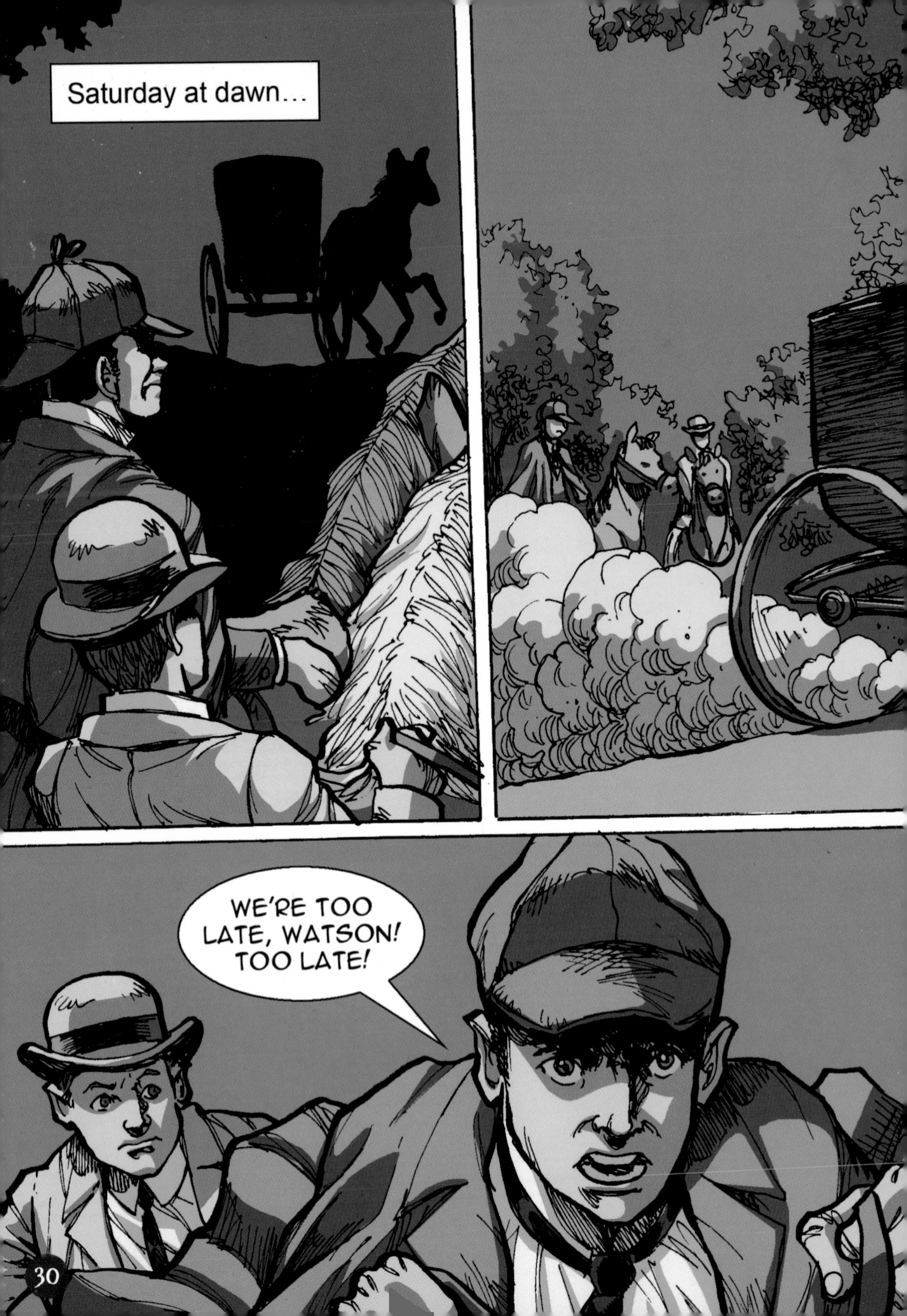
Saturday at dawn…
WE'RE TOO LATE, WATSON! TOO LATE!

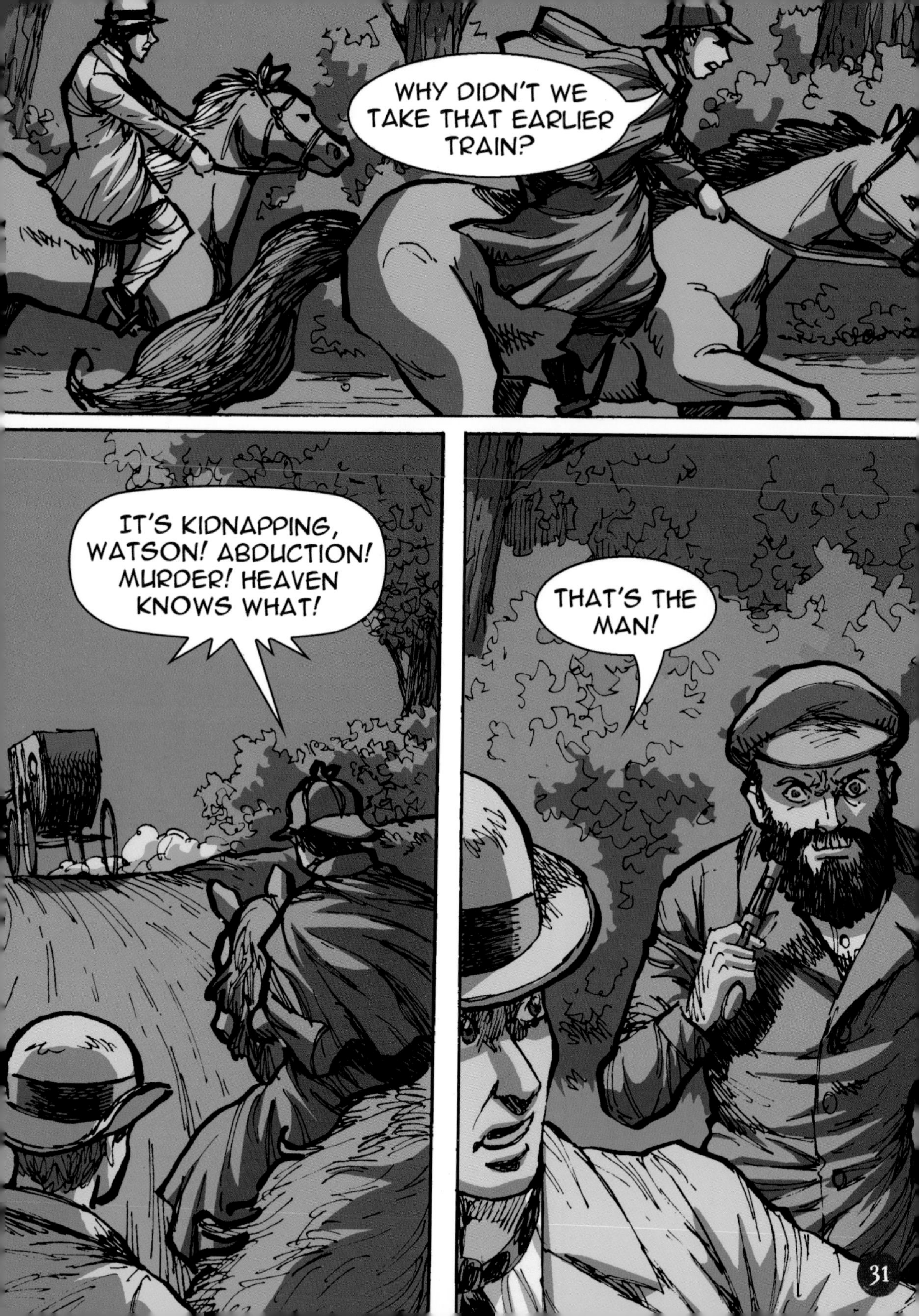
WHY DIDN'T WE TAKE THAT EARLIER TRAIN?
IT'S KIDNAPPING, WATSON! ABDUCTION! MURDER! HEAVEN KNOWS WHAT!
THAT'S THE MAN!

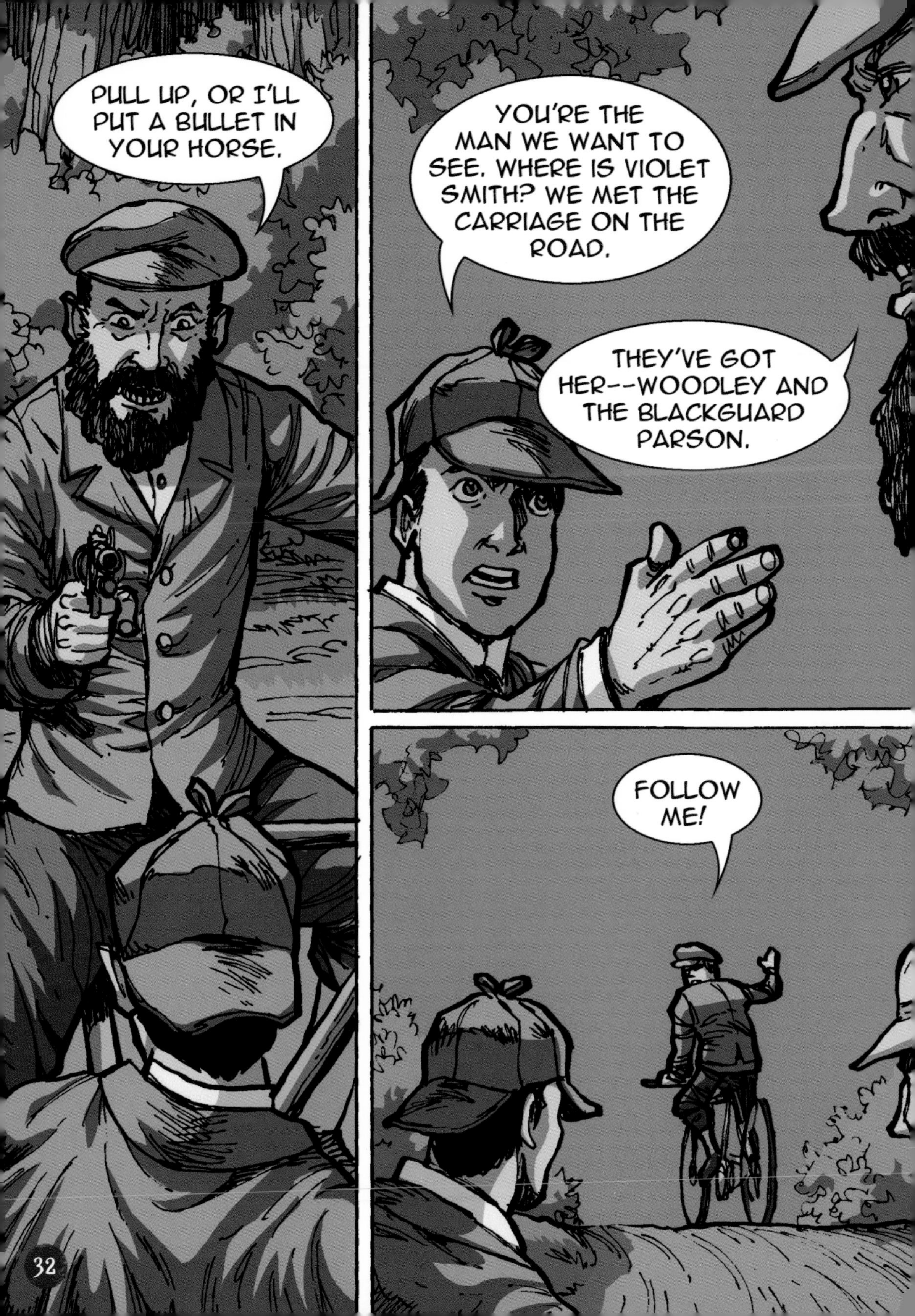
PULL UP, OR I'LL PUT A BULLET IN YOUR HORSE.
YOU'RE THE MAN WE WANT TO SEE. WHERE IS VIOLET SMITH? WE MET THE CARRIAGE ON THE ROAD.
THEY'VE GOT HER--WOODLEY AND THE BLACKGUARD PARSON.
FOLLOW ME!

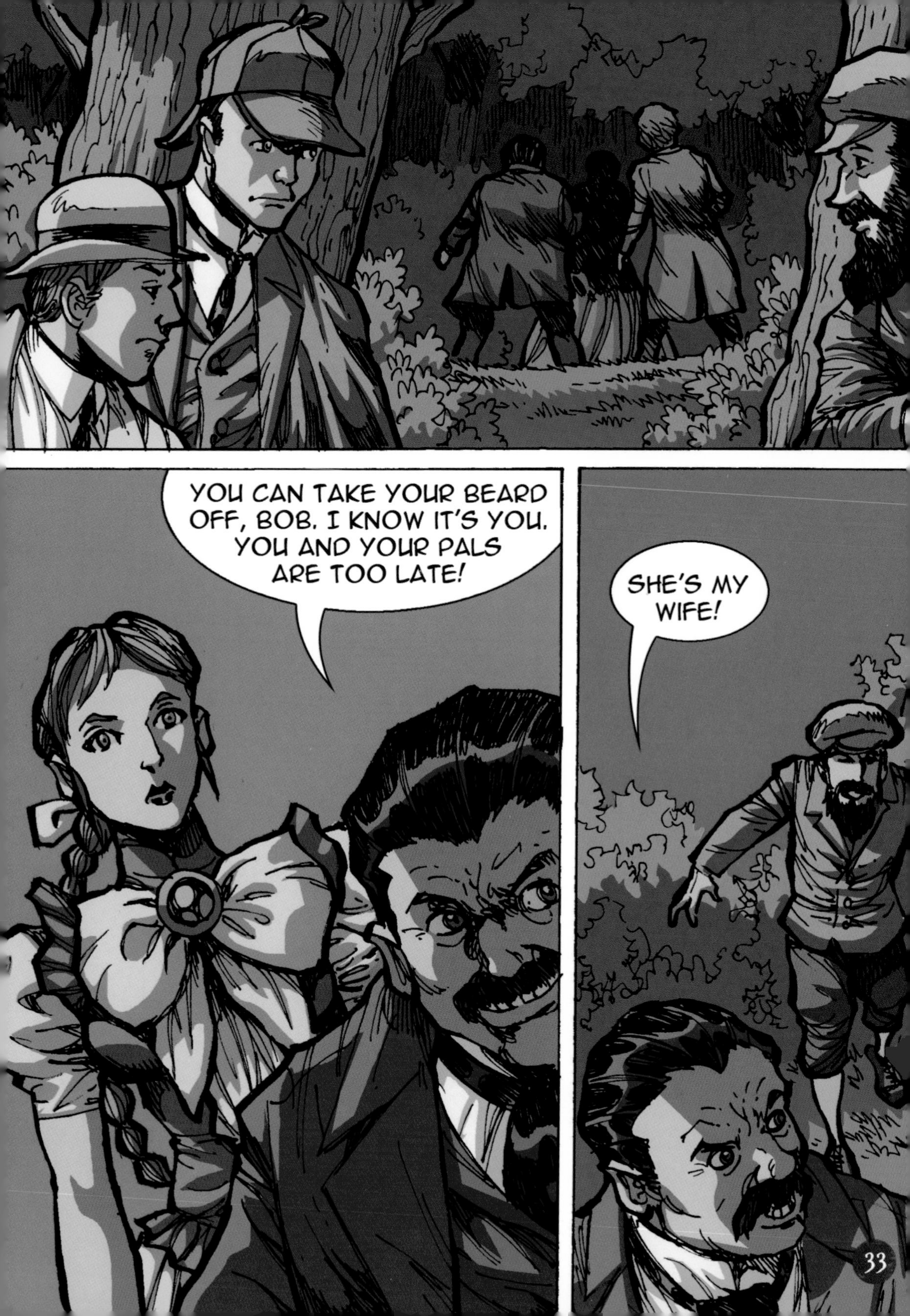
YOU CAN TAKE YOUR BEARD OFF, BOB. I KNOW IT'S YOU. YOU AND YOUR PALS ARE TOO LATE!
SHE'S MY WIFE!

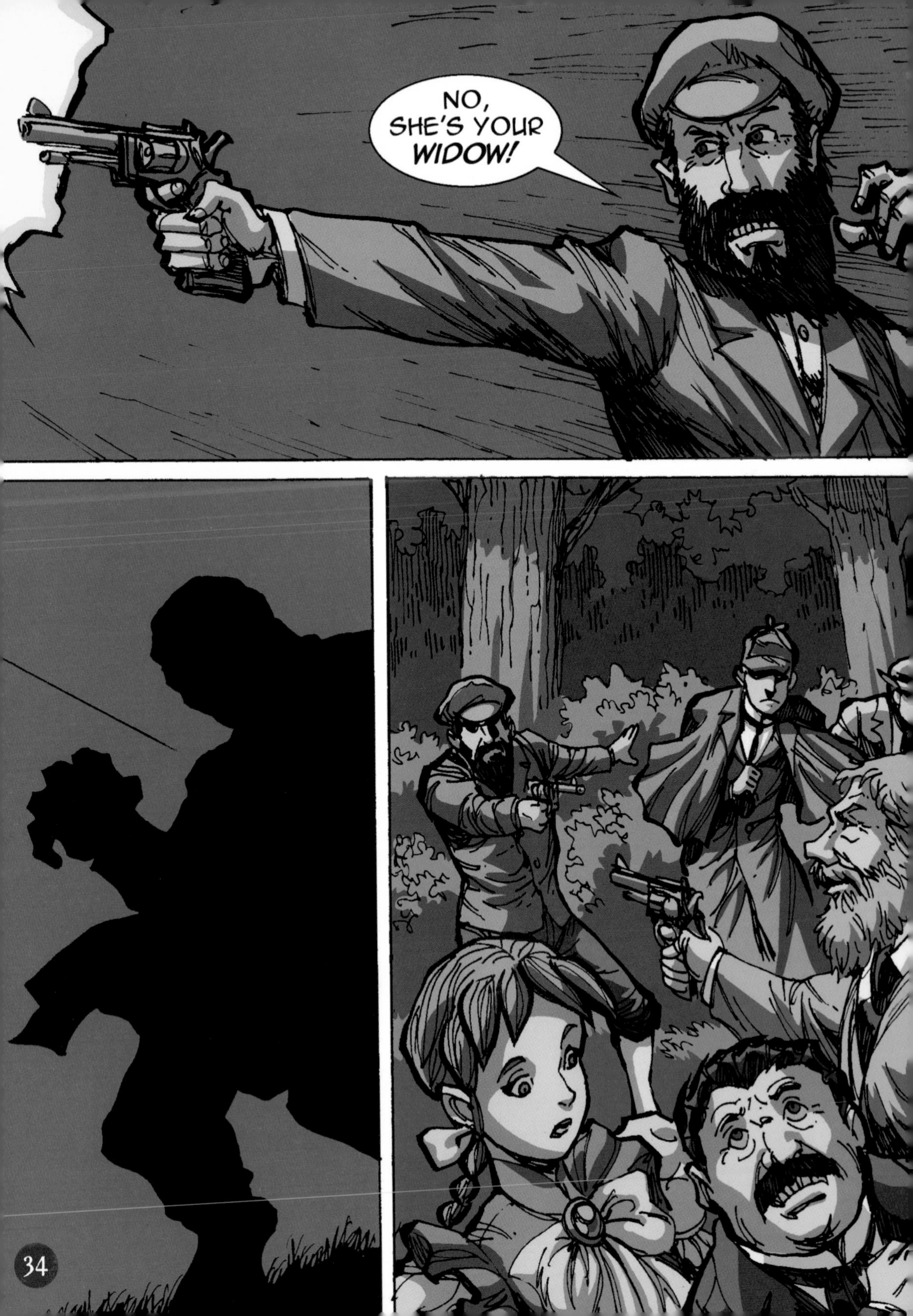
NO,
SHE'S YOUR
WIDOW!

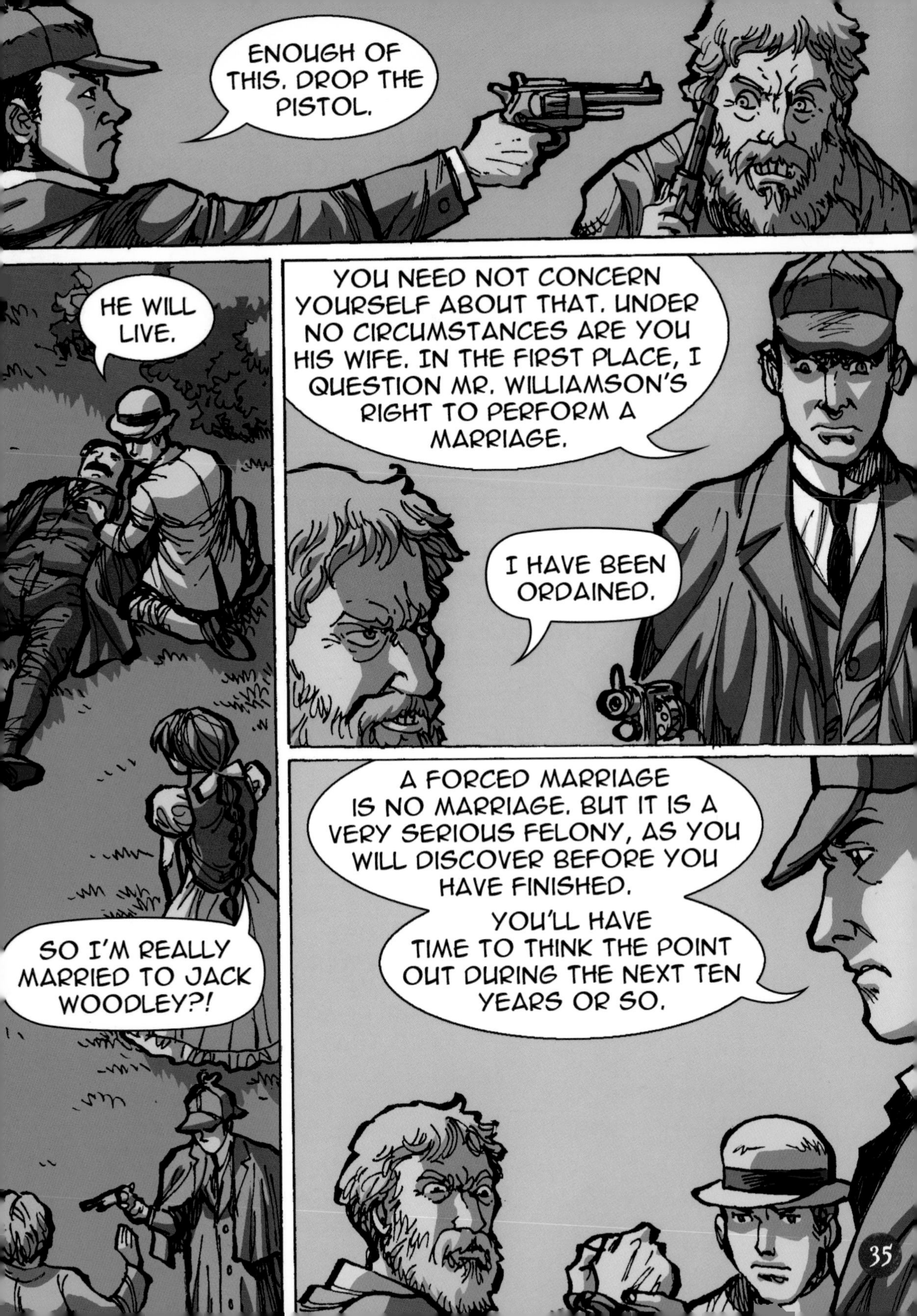
ENOUGH OF THIS. DROP THE PISTOL.
HE WILL LIVE.
YOU NEED NOT CONCERN YOURSELF ABOUT THAT. UNDER NO CIRCUMSTANCES ARE YOU HIS WIFE. IN THE FIRST PLACE, I QUESTION MR. WILLIAMSON'S RIGHT TO PERFORM A MARRIAGE.
I HAVE BEEN ORDAINED.
SO I'M REALLY MARRIED TO JACK WOODLEY?!
A FORCED MARRIAGE IS NO MARRIAGE. BUT IT IS A VERY SERIOUS FELONY, AS YOU WILL DISCOVER BEFORE YOU HAVE FINISHED.
YOU'LL HAVE TIME TO THINK THE POINT OUT DURING THE NEXT TEN YEARS OR SO.

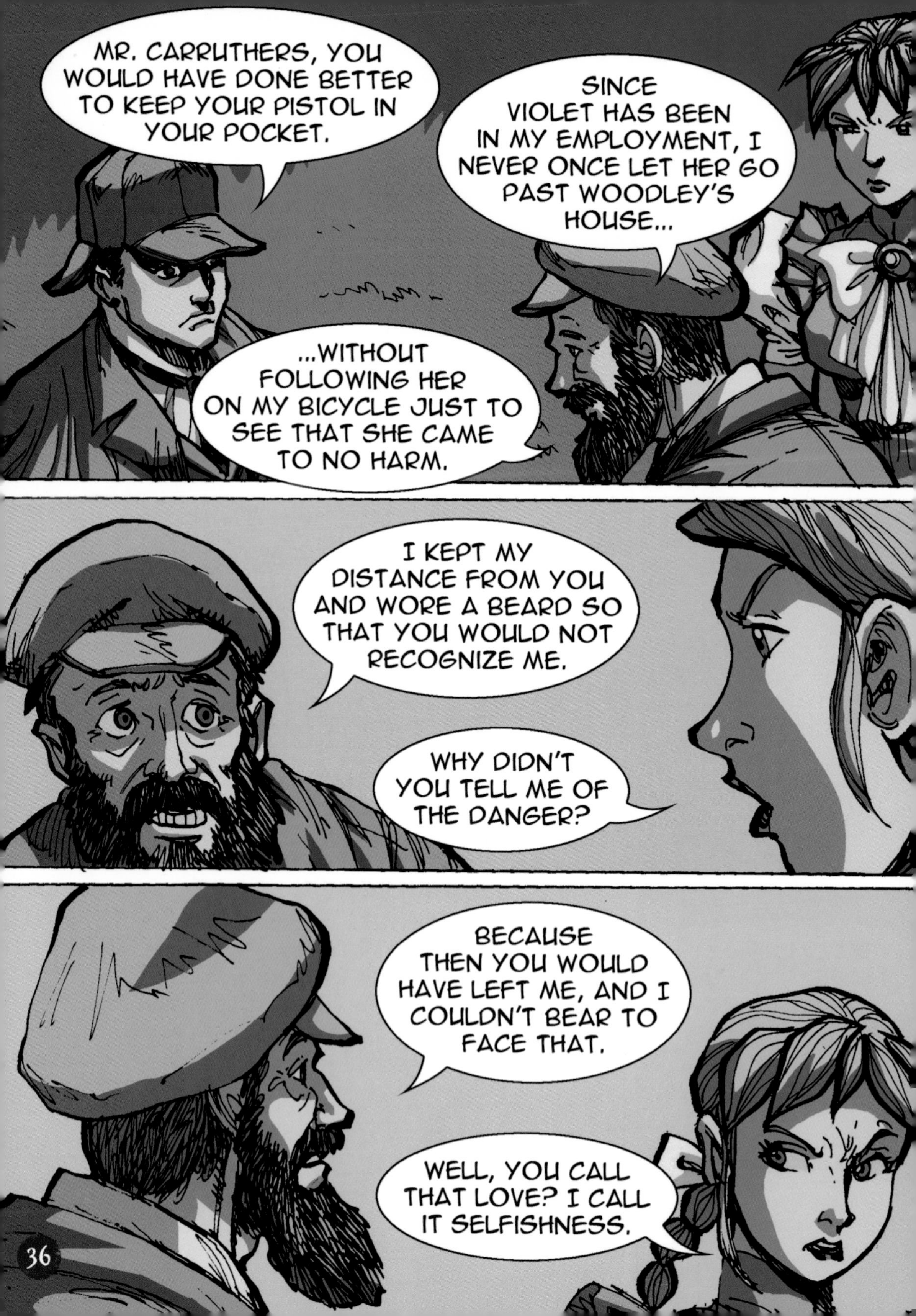
MR. CARRUTHERS, YOU WOULD HAVE DONE BETTER TO KEEP YOUR PISTOL IN YOUR POCKET.
SINCE VIOLET HAS BEEN IN MY EMPLOYMENT, I NEVER ONCE LET HER GO PAST WOODLEY'S HOUSE...
...WITHOUT FOLLOWING HER ON MY BICYCLE JUST TO SEE THAT SHE CAME TO NO HARM.
I KEPT MY DISTANCE FROM YOU AND WORE A BEARD SO THAT YOU WOULD NOT RECOGNIZE ME.
WHY DIDN'T YOU TELL ME OF THE DANGER?
BECAUSE THEN YOU WOULD HAVE LEFT ME, AND I COULDN'T BEAR TO FACE THAT.
WELL, YOU CALL THAT LOVE? I CALL IT SELFISHNESS.

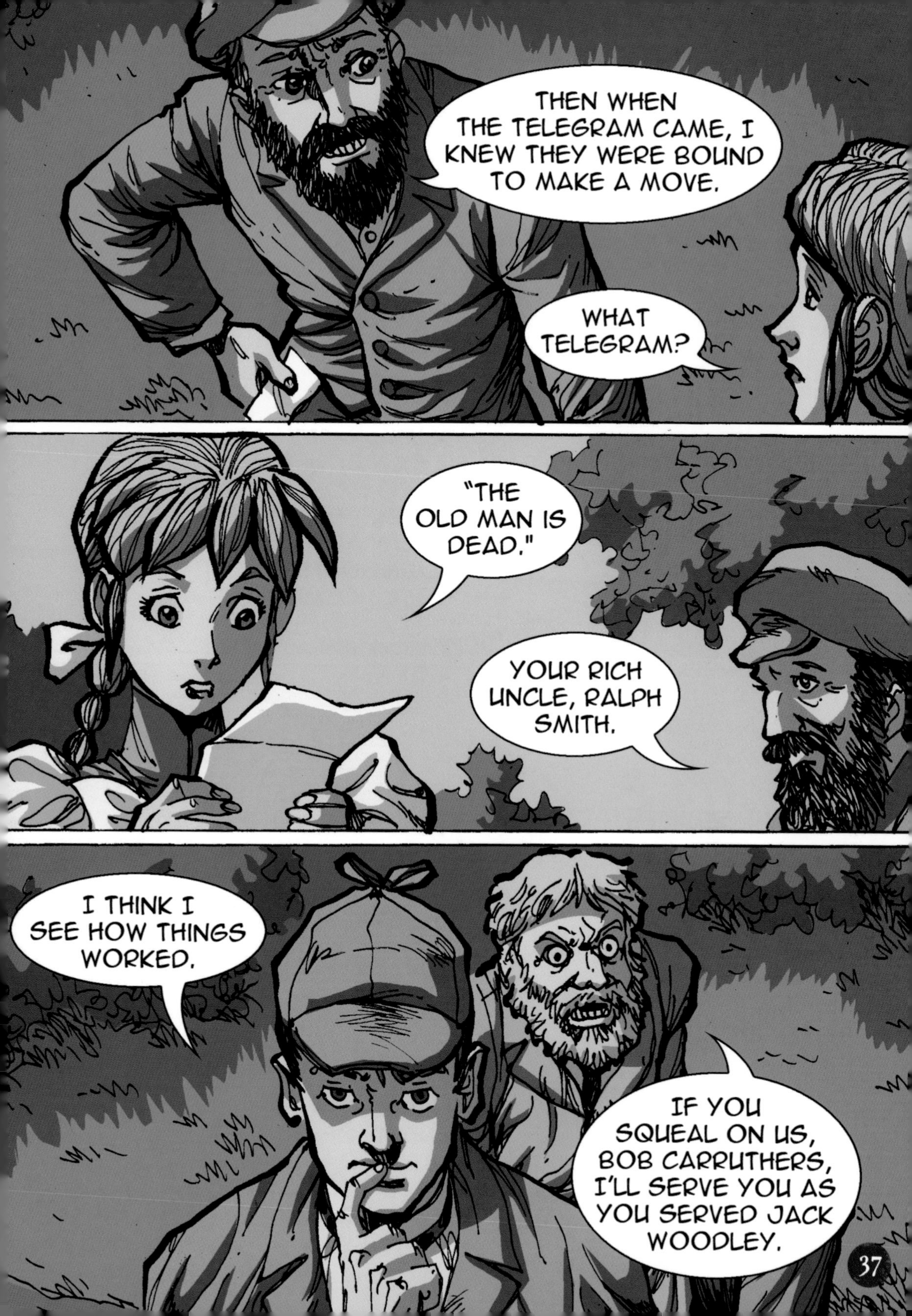

THEN WHEN THE TELEGRAM CAME, I KNEW THEY WERE BOUND TO MAKE A MOVE.
WHAT TELEGRAM?
"THE OLD MAN IS DEAD."
YOUR RICH UNCLE, RALPH SMITH.
I THINK I SEE HOW THINGS WORKED.
IF YOU SQUEAL ON US, BOB CARRUTHERS, I'LL SERVE YOU AS YOU SERVED JACK WOODLEY.

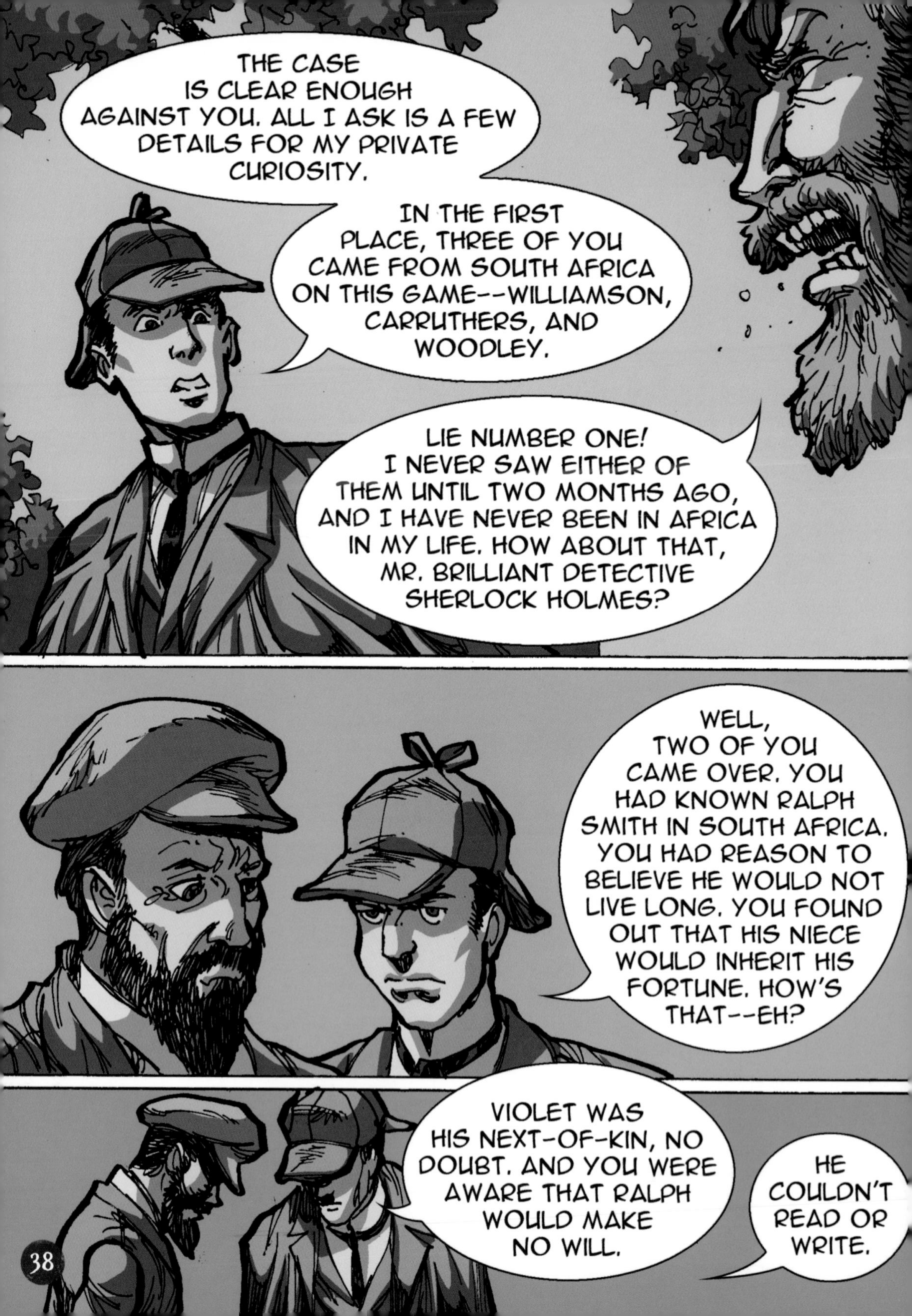
THE CASE IS CLEAR ENOUGH AGAINST YOU. ALL I ASK IS A FEW DETAILS FOR MY PRIVATE CURIOSITY.
IN THE FIRST PLACE, THREE OF YOU CAME FROM SOUTH AFRICA ON THIS GAME--WILLIAMSON, CARRUTHERS, AND WOODLEY.
LIE NUMBER ONE! I NEVER SAW EITHER OF THEM UNTIL TWO MONTHS AGO, AND I HAVE NEVER BEEN IN AFRICA IN MY LIFE. HOW ABOUT THAT, MR. BRILLIANT DETECTIVE SHERLOCK HOLMES?
WELL, TWO OF YOU CAME OVER. YOU HAD KNOWN RALPH SMITH IN SOUTH AFRICA. YOU HAD REASON TO BELIEVE HE WOULD NOT LIVE LONG. YOU FOUND OUT THAT HIS NIECE WOULD INHERIT HIS FORTUNE. HOW'S THAT--EH?
VIOLET WAS HIS NEXT-OF-KIN, NO DOUBT. AND YOU WERE AWARE THAT RALPH WOULD MAKE NO WILL.
HE COULDN'T READ OR WRITE.

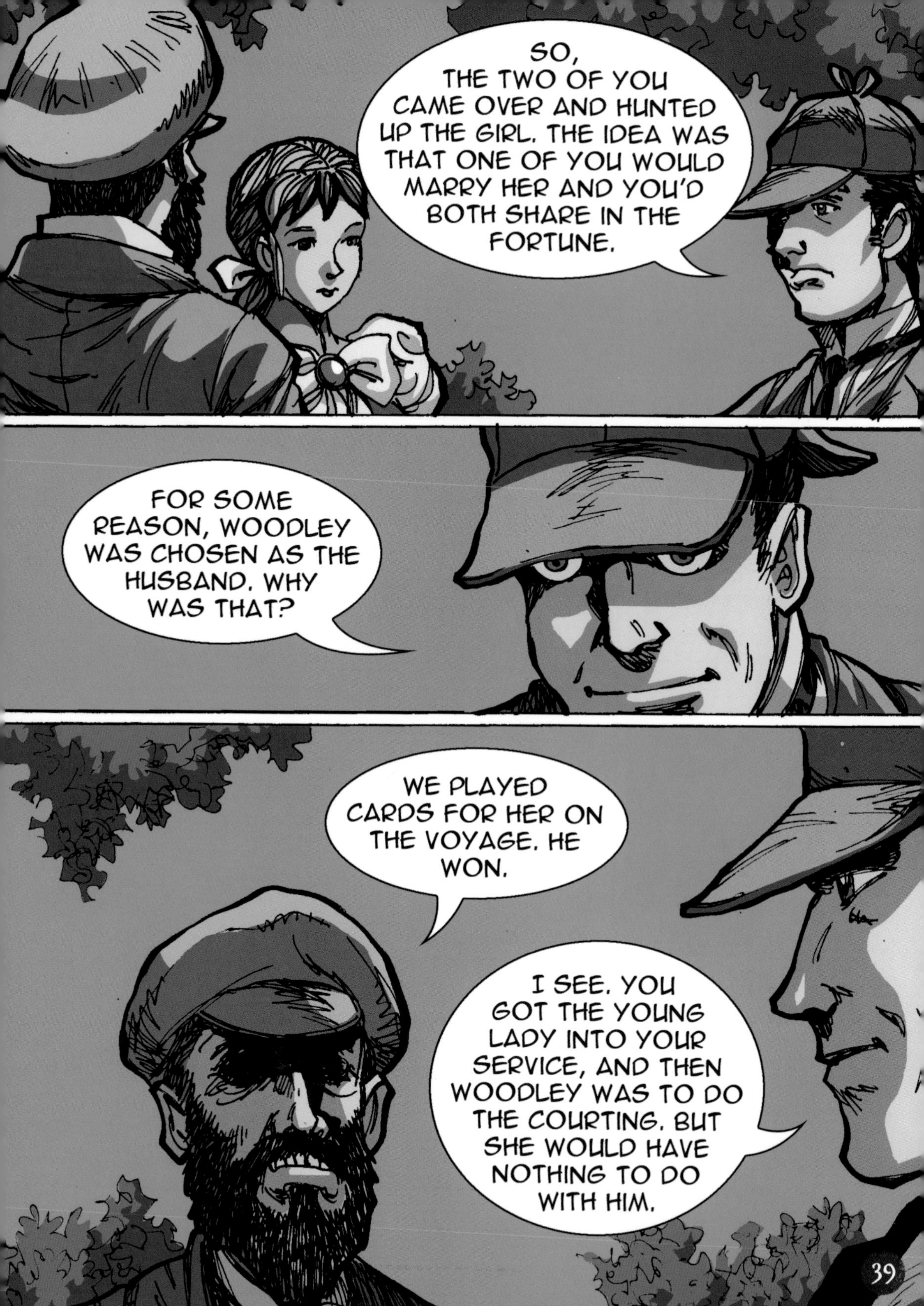
SO, THE TWO OF YOU CAME OVER AND HUNTED UP THE GIRL. THE IDEA WAS THAT ONE OF YOU WOULD MARRY HER AND YOU'D BOTH SHARE IN THE FORTUNE.
FOR SOME REASON, WOODLEY WAS CHOSEN AS THE HUSBAND. WHY WAS THAT?
WE PLAYED CARDS FOR HER ON THE VOYAGE. HE WON.
I SEE. YOU GOT THE YOUNG LADY INTO YOUR SERVICE, AND THEN WOODLEY WAS TO DO THE COURTING. BUT SHE WOULD HAVE NOTHING TO DO WITH HIM.

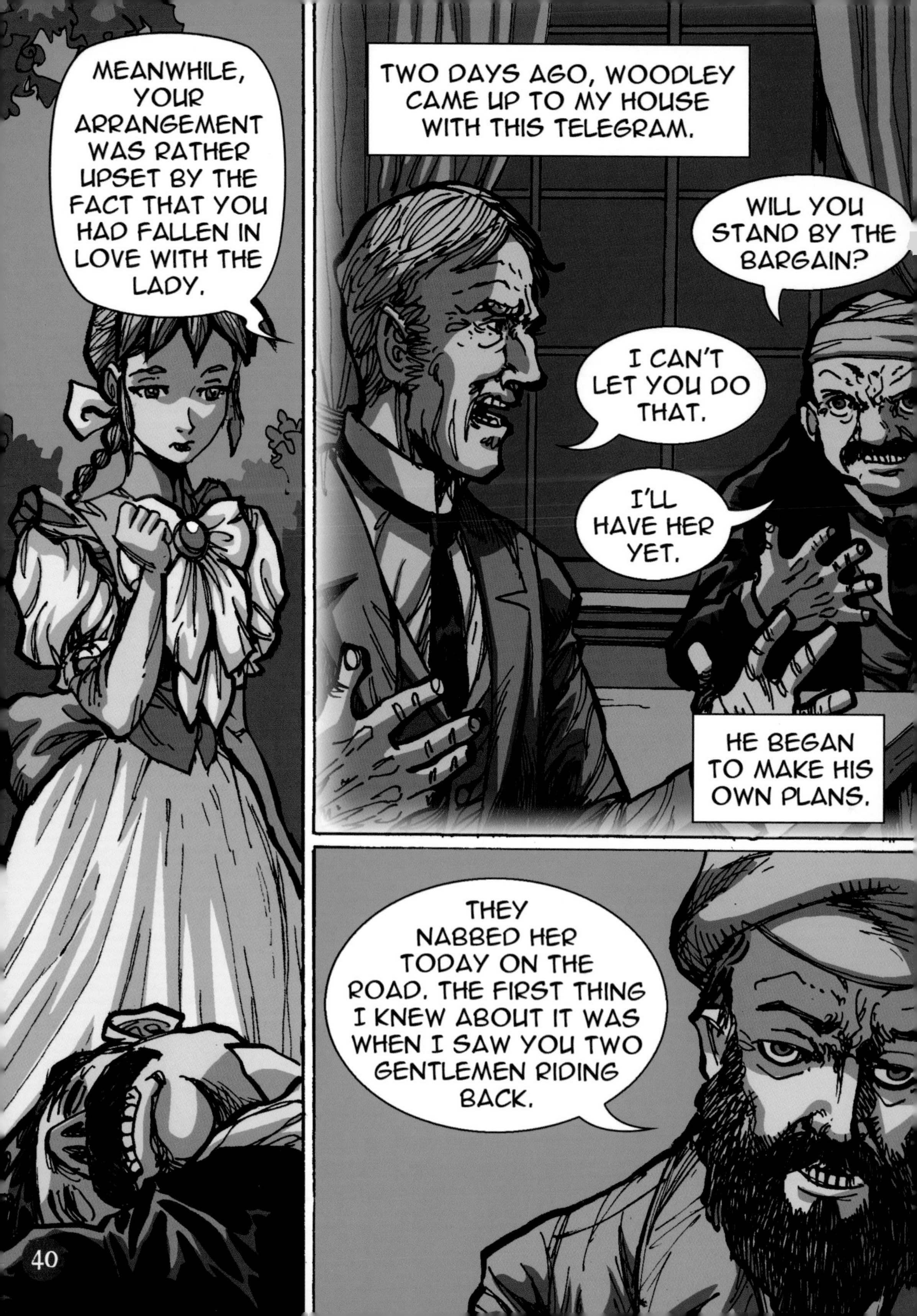
MEANWHILE, YOUR ARRANGEMENT WAS RATHER UPSET BY THE FACT THAT YOU HAD FALLEN IN LOVE WITH THE LADY.
TWO DAYS AGO, WOODLEY CAME UP TO MY HOUSE WITH THIS TELEGRAM.
WILL YOU STAND BY THE BARGAIN?
I CAN'T LET YOU DO THAT.
I'LL HAVE HER YET.
HE BEGAN TO MAKE HIS OWN PLANS.
THEY NABBED HER TODAY ON THE ROAD. THE FIRST THING I KNEW ABOUT IT WAS WHEN I SAW YOU TWO GENTLEMEN RIDING BACK.

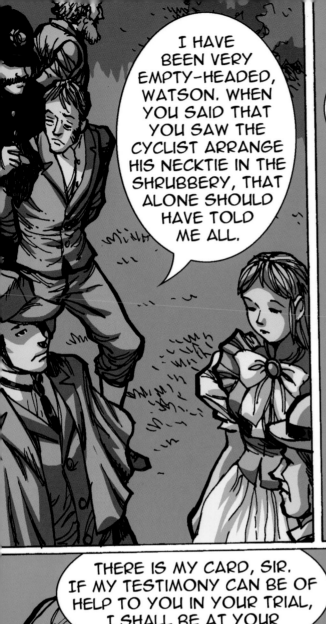

I HAVE BEEN VERY EMPTY-HEADED, WATSON. WHEN YOU SAID THAT YOU SAW THE CYCLIST ARRANGE HIS NECKTIE IN THE SHRUBBERY, THAT ALONE SHOULD HAVE TOLD ME ALL.

MR. CARRUTHERS, I THINK THAT YOU HAVE DONE WHAT YOU COULD TO MAKE AMENDS FOR YOUR SHARE IN AN EVIL PLOT.

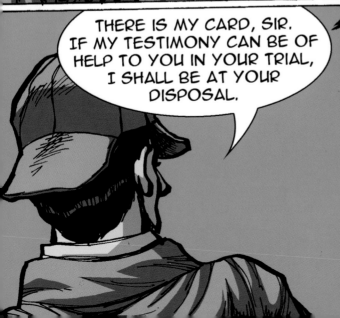

THERE IS MY CARD, SIR. IF MY TESTIMONY CAN BE OF HELP TO YOU IN YOUR TRIAL, I SHALL BE AT YOUR DISPOSAL.

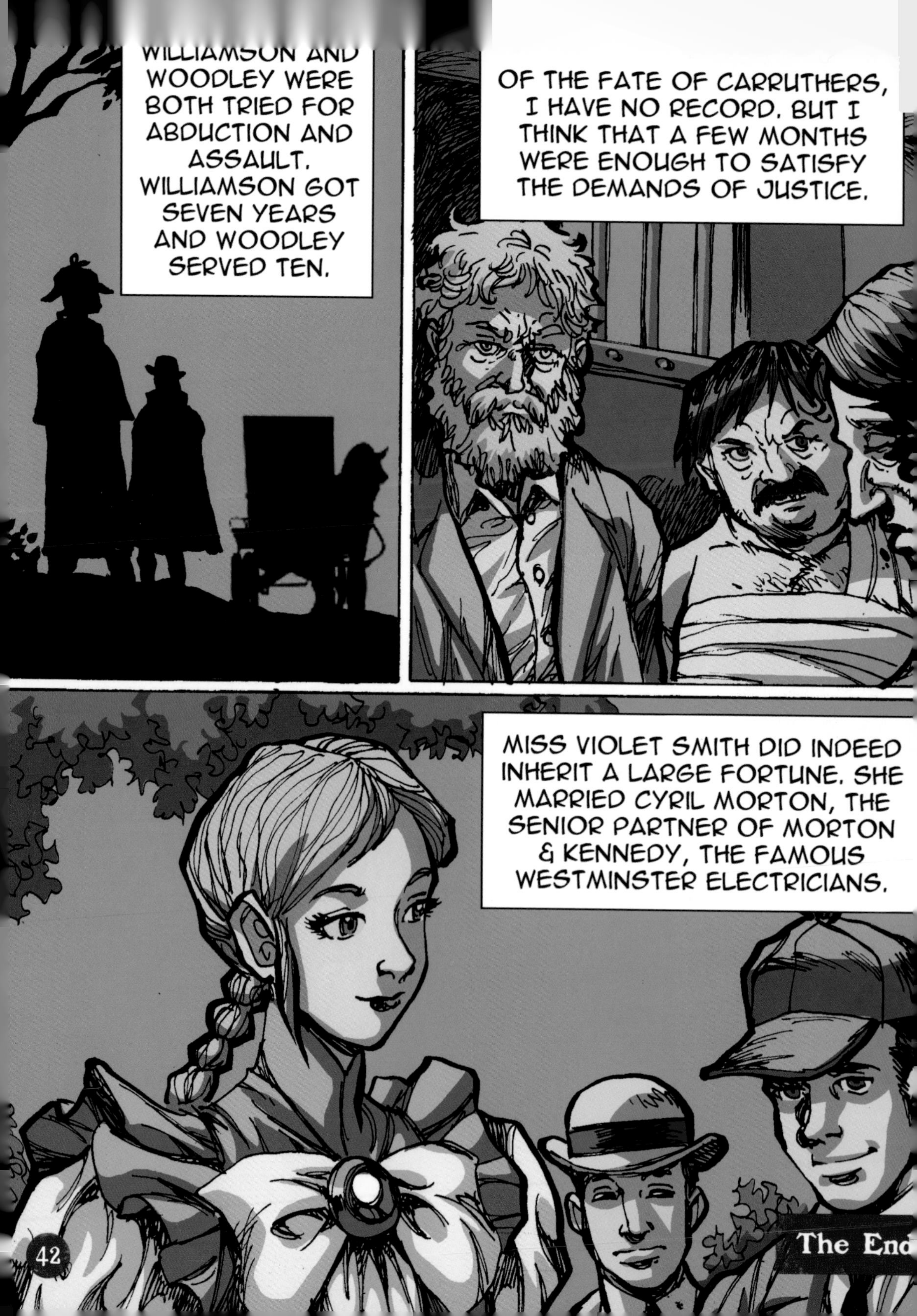
WILLIAMSON AND WOODLEY WERE BOTH TRIED FOR ABDUCTION AND ASSAULT. WILLIAMSON GOT SEVEN YEARS AND WOODLEY SERVED TEN.
OF THE FATE OF CARRUTHERS, I HAVE NO RECORD. BUT I THINK THAT A FEW MONTHS WERE ENOUGH TO SATISFY THE DEMANDS OF JUSTICE.
MISS VIOLET SMITH DID INDEED INHERIT A LARGE FORTUNE. SHE MARRIED CYRIL MORTON, THE SENIOR PARTNER OF MORTON & KENNEDY, THE FAMOUS WESTMINSTER ELECTRICIANS.
The End

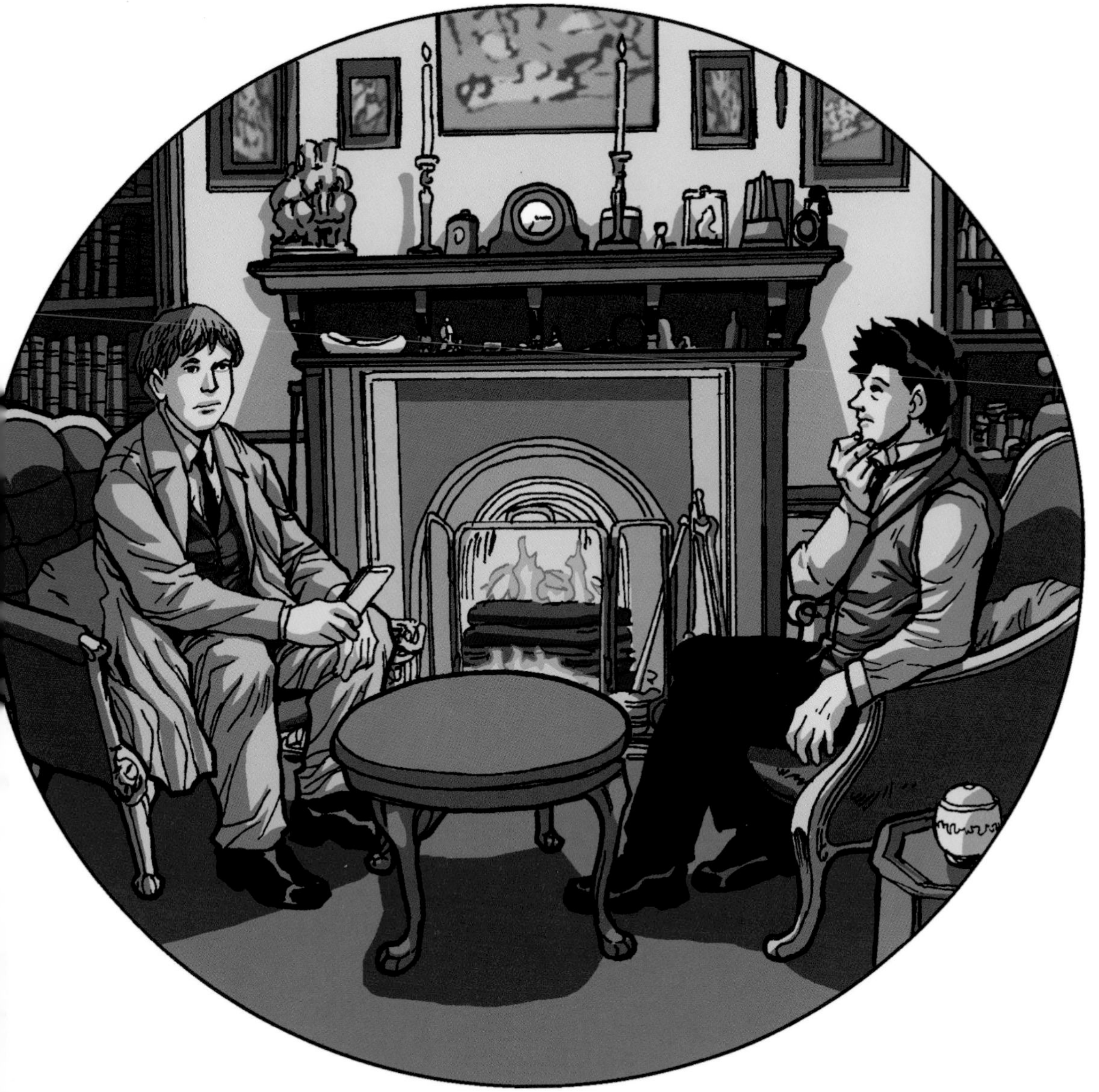

How to Draw
Sherlock Holmes

by Ben Dunn

Step 1: Use a pencil to draw a simple framework. You can start with a stick figure! Then add circles, ovals, and cylinders to get the basic form. Getting the simple shapes in place is the beginning to solving any great case.

Step 2: Time to add to Sherlock's look. Use the shapes you started with to fill in his clothes. Use guidelines to add circles for the eyes. And don't forget the hair.

Step 3: Now you can go in with a pen and start inking Sherlock. Fill in all the details and fix any mistakes. Let the ink dry to avoid smudges, then erase any pencil marks. Sherlock is ready for some color, so grab your markers and get started!

Glossary

associate - connected or having equal rank.

bizarre - very strange or out of the ordinary.

blackguard - a rude or evil person.

circumstances - conditions at a certain time or place.

curiosity - the state of being interested in something unusual or strange.

discomfort - something that makes one uncomfortable or uneasy.

elimination - to get rid of or remove.

felony - a grave crime that gets stronger punishment.

inherit - to receive money or belongings passed on to someone after a person dies.

inquiry - an investigation in a matter of public interest.

insult - to treat someone offensively.

keen - eager.

odious - causing hatred or strong dislike.

ordained - having officially been made a minister or a priest.

pound - an English coin equal to 12 shillings. Twelve shillings weigh one pound (.5 kg).

responsible - able to be relied on for something; dependable.

situation - the state of a person's wealth or employment.

testimony - a statement given by someone under oath to tell the truth.

Web Sites

To learn more about Sir Arthur Conan Doyle, visit ABDO Group online at **www.abdopublishing.com**. Web sites about Doyle are featured on our Book Links page. These links are routinely monitored and updated to provide the most current information available.

About the Author

Arthur Conan Doyle was born on May 22, 1859, in Edinburgh, Scotland. He was the second of Charles Altamont and Mary Foley Doyle's ten children. In 1868, Doyle began his schooling in England. Eight years later, he returned to Scotland.

Upon his return, Doyle entered the University of Edinburgh's medical school, where he became a doctor in 1885. That year, he married Louisa Hawkins. Together they had two children.

While a medical student, Doyle was impressed when his professor observed the tiniest details of a patient's condition. Doyle later wrote stories where his most famous character, Sherlock Holmes, used this same technique to solve mysteries. Holmes first appeared in *A Study in Scarlet* in 1887 and was immediately popular.

Between 1887 and 1927, Doyle wrote 66 stories and 3 novels about Holmes. He also wrote other fiction and nonfiction novels throughout his life. In 1902, Doyle was knighted for his work in a field hospital in the South African War. Four years later, Louisa died. Doyle married Jean Leckie in 1907, and they had three children together.

Sir Arthur Conan Doyle died on July 7, 1930, in Sussex, England. Today, Doyle's famous character, Sherlock Holmes, is honored with societies around the world that pay tribute to the detective.

Additional Works

A Study in Scarlet (1887)

The Mystery of Cloomber (1889)

The Firm of Girdlestone (1890)

The White Company (1891)

The Adventures of Sherlock Holmes (1891-92)

The Memoirs of Sherlock Holmes (1892-93)

Round the Red Lamp (1894)

The Stark Munro Letters (1895)

The Great Boer War (1900)

The Hound of the Baskervilles (1901-02)

The Return of Sherlock Holmes (1903-04)

Through the Magic Door (1907)

The Crime of the Congo (1909)

The Coming of the Fairies (1922)

Memories and Adventures (1924)

The Case-Book of Sherlock Holmes (1921-27)

About the Adapters

Author

Vincent Goodwin earned his BA in Drama and Communications from Trinity University in San Antonio. He is the writer of three plays as well as the cowriter of the comic book *Pirates vs. Ninjas II*. Goodwin is also an accomplished journalist, having won several awards for his work as a columnist and reporter.

Illustrator

Ben Dunn founded Antarctic Press, one of the largest comic companies in the United States. His works appear in Marvel and Image comics. He is best known for his series *Ninja High School* and *Warrior Nun Areala*.